SURVIVING HUMANITY

A WRITEHIVE ANTHOLOGY

This is a collection of fictional works. Names, characters, places, and incidents are either a product of the author's imagination or are used fictitiously. Any resemblance to actual persons, living or dead, businesses, companies, events, or locales, is entirely coincidental.

Surviving Humanity

Inked in Gray Press

InkedinGray.com

Copyright © 2026

All rights reserved.

ISBN Paperback: 978-1-952969-46-1

ISBN Ebook: 978-1-952969-47-8

Cover Design by MIBLArts

A WRITEHIVE ANTHOLOGY
SURVIVING
HUMANITY

Contents

Foreword

Growing up in SoCal, not far from Los Angeles, smog was an ever-present part of life. The yellow haze marred most of our blue skies and obscured the mountains surrounding the valley from view. We used to joke about getting "all our minerals in one breath." But those same breaths would burn lungs and exacerbate health conditions, such as asthma. There are some who complain now about regulations, but I remember how bad it was, and I have seen in other countries how bad it can get. I am grateful that regulations are there to keep our skies bluer and our air cleaner.

I am far from an environmental expert, but there are two things I've learned that have proven true over and over again: What humans do impact everything around them and those with unchecked power will not leave a positive impact.

Humans are consistently, throughout history and across the globe, the worst enemy of themselves and the earth. Every war, every bomb dropped, every oil spill, every enslavement has humans behind it, drunk on the lie of superiority or greed. But death doesn't care about titles or race or bank accounts, and all that truly remains are the people impacted.

Those people are more likely the ones reading this anthology. Like me, you're angry and distressed about the world around you. Chances are, you've been a victim of the system of your country or the bigots that live within it. One in three women experience violence of one form or another at least once in their lives. The LGBTQ+ community is 5 times more likely to be victims of violent crimes. Add to that the difficulties receiving adequate healthcare, physically or mentally, and it's easy to feel hopeless or helpless in this world.

But humans are more than our destructive nature. Even in the most desperate times, there are people reaching out to help. People who refuse to give up. People who actually care. People who stand up to tyranny despite threats to their lives or worse. While I do not have faith in humanity, I do believe in the power of love and truth to outshine the hate and lies that so often obscure our lives.

So I want you to know that you are loved and you are not alone. The kindness you show others, the times you protest on the behalf of those whose rights are being trampled, or even just simply the times you care about the world around you, it is not in vain. An encouraging word gets someone through a difficult day. Standing up against injustice gives others the courage to do the same. Even if positive change is not realized in our lifetimes, it will be someday if we persist.

I hope these stories help give you some inspiration or strength to keep surviving.

Jerusha René (she/her), WriteHive CEO

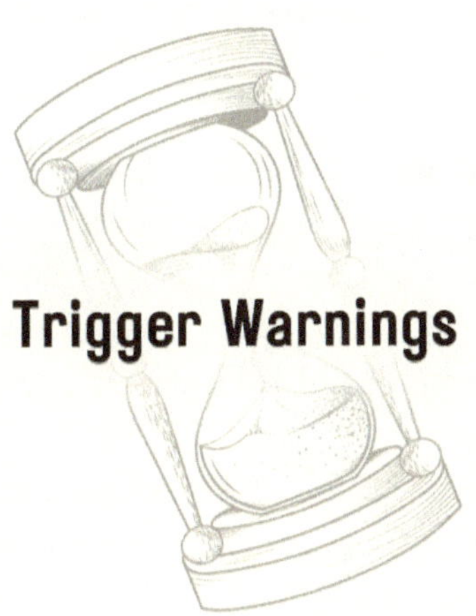

Trigger Warnings

The following are the content warnings for *Surviving Humanity*. If you don't like to read content warnings, that's fine! Please skip this page and read on.

Otherwise, know that this book contains content that could be difficult for some readers. Below are the stories and their associated content:

The Melancholy Woodwinder: violence, war

If You're Reading This, You're Still Alive: mental health, chronic illness, severe depression/anxiety, discussion of suicide/suicidal thoughts, eating disorder, death

The Lucky One: attempted suicide, gun violence, animal death, gore, terminal illness

Roiling Waves: horror elements (death, violence)

Emmaline: child injury, child death, hospital scenes,

medical scenes, mentions of surgery, mentions of car accidents

Men's Disease: war, mass death, disease

Dark Matters: Violence

Primary Objective: end of humanity, human sexuality

Please feel free to reach out at contact@inkedingray.com for any clarifying questions or concerns and remember to take care of your mental health.
You matter.

The Melancholy Woodwinder

by Susan L. Lin

EACH DAY, I wake an hour before my alarm, the last phantasms of sleep evaporating from my body as the melancholy woodwinder plays his mournful song on the street below my bedroom window. Somewhere deep inside my chest cavity, I recognize that tune. I cannot place it in my memory, and yet, I know intuitively that it's a song without a title, the kind of song that relishes these pre-dawn hours, hides under the cover of the morning mist, hopes to never be found out. The name of this sorrowful instrument eludes me, too. A clarinet, I wonder? An oboe? Or maybe a bassoon? I am no expert, but I have long yearned to understand the secret history behind such soulful notes.

One foggy day, the melancholy woodwinder is still performing as I exit my building to float about the hazy neighborhood, a ghost in a white maxi dress. I'm surprised to find a slight girl, red ribbons curled in her hair, leaning against a brick wall in the alley. I've never before seen the musical instrument that waits patiently between her lips for the next command: It's shaped like a hatchet but with a blade fashioned out of whittled wood, its thick handle drilled with careful holes. The agile fingers that tap dance along its unvarnished surface belong to a prodigy, her prized possession a family heirloom passed down for many generations. It was handcrafted by her great-great-grandmother during the last world war, she tells me.

A tool at rest doesn't yet realize its whole purpose. The hatchet, for example, becomes a violent weapon in the wrong hands. In the right ones, it can transform into an evocative woodwind. But learning how to coax pleasant sounds from its body of timber is a lifelong pursuit. *What's that song you're always playing?* I ask the girl. *It's an old one*, she says. *We're both too young to remember its true origins.* Nevertheless, as she refills her elastic lungs with a slow inhale, I feel the weight of past decades and centuries collecting within my own ribcage. And when she blows her warm breath back into that precious hatchet, I swear I can see the long exhale of our ancestors as nearby trees stretch their limbs overhead like yogis, scattering colored leaves.

About Susan L. Lin

Susan L. Lin is a Taiwanese American storyteller who hails from southeast Texas and holds an MFA in Writing from California College of the Arts. Her novella GOODBYE TO THE OCEAN won the 2022 Etchings Press novella prize, and her short prose and poetry have appeared in over fifty different publications. She loves to dance. Find more on Twitter @SusanLLin, on Instagram @susanlinosaur, Bluesky @susanllin.bsky.social or on the web at https://susanllin.com.

If You're Reading This, You're Still Alive

by Jake Stein

AS A SURVIVOR, it's hard to admit that I want to die. But that's just what the Fog does to people.

Take me, for instance. This skinny, foul-smelling, sad sack of . . . you get it. Currently, I'm searching the snack food aisle for the will to live. Took me a few starving days to work up the nerve, but here I am, in another grocery store where the lights are too bright.

I reach for a small bag of kettle chips.

Contact . . . unsuccessful.

My hand, that numb and pale piece of me, drops limply to my side, as empty as I feel. Deflected by some invisible, insurmountable barrier.

The fluorescent lights blare like stars against this tile floor. I'd very much like, under different circumstances, to curl up on that cheap white linoleum, to hide from the brightness and hold my breath forever, because I can't find my appetite, much less the meaning of existence, in a bag of chips.

My sweaty shirt clings to me like a stain as I head for the door. "Pointless," I'm saying to myself, about myself, drowning so deep in my own world that a random act of kindness nearly eludes me.

This door isn't automatic. I would have run directly into it, face-first, if not for the smiling stranger holding it for me.

I look up, mustering my manners. "Thanks very much."

The stranger stares — even *smiles* — at me. "You might as well just get it over with," she says, perfectly polite. "Go die and be done with it. There's a bridge up the street, if you have a mind to jump. Otherwise, you could buy some sleeping pills from the pharmacy and chug the whole bottle . . ."

It takes everything, and I mean everything, not to scream as I run — and I mean *run* — away. Scream because I know that's not what she actually said, but it's what I actually heard. Because the Fog will never stop clogging my ears, let alone my brain, with lies that sound more honest than reality, more true than life.

The day is getting too hot to move through. Emaciated muscles protest with burning cramps. Huffing heavy air, weeping sweat, I take stock of my surroundings. I would kill for a Gatorade. That, or a handful of pills. But I've walked down this road plenty of times before; I've even sobbed here before. So I know there aren't any drug stores nearby.

But rising over not-too-distant rooftops, the arch of a bridge shines like polished gold beneath the sun.

It's not like I've been planning for a while to jump off this bridge in particular. There are plenty of bridges in the world. This just happened to be closest.

My feet pull me along. My hand skims the rusty railing, hopping over the occasional smear of pigeon shit. I don't stop until I'm at the highest point, and the river is a sparkling invitation hundreds of feet below.

I wonder how much of a difference it would make, at this height, at such speed, to hit water, versus . . . say, concrete. Would the bone-breakage turn out to be comparable?

Would you drown, or would the sheer blunt force do the trick?

One last breath. The air stings my insides. I look down and the river beckons. What am I waiting for?

I take another last breath. And another.

A passing car honks. A bird flaps overhead.

It's only a border. Only the crossing of a line between this and that. Nothing could be simpler . . . nothing easier . . .

But the easiness of the thing is what scares me. Nothing good comes easily in life, and I doubt death is any different. For instance, what if this fall isn't the end? What if, by trying to escape my pain, I dive straight into an even worse nightmare?

Putting the afterlife aside, I force a smile, making a genuine effort to appreciate these final seconds. Trying to be, just be, for once. But that's the problem: If I'm already here to begin with — thinking, breathing, swaying in the wind — then why is it so damn difficult to *be here to begin with*?

The song of the birds and the city — that dissonant duet which, in another life, I used to whistle along with — doesn't help, and neither does the gorgeous day, because I know none of it will last — not me, not the summer, not even the sun itself.

In the long run, everything burns out.

From the corner of my vision, a string of spray-painted graffiti on the sidewalk catches my eye. Squinting against the brightness of the world, I read it, then read it again, that trampled, faded message. Unless I'm hallucinating — which is definitely possible — it says:

If you're reading this, you're still alive.

My indignant response to the sidewalk: "You're right, but only technically."

Closing my eyes and closing my soul, I climb halfway over the railing. I can practically taste the river already. The rushing wind, the blood, the last bit of pain . . . But I can taste something else too. I can taste the nothingness, the stale lack of anything, that empty eternity I'm about to throw myself willingly into. The taste of forever — or rather, the taste of *never again*.

The sidewalk's message returns to me, spoken by a small, unfamiliar voice between my ears: *Still alive* . . .

Sucking swampy heat, I climb back down. Soon enough I'm leaving the bridge the way it was intended to be left, without shortcuts. Yes, I'm walking away from death — but only for the meantime, and not because some old graffiti saved me. Not entirely, at least.

Because, despite the fact that I didn't jump, I just can't convince myself that I'm really living.

The sun is still stuck in the sky when I shamble up to a numbered sign. It appears to be a bus stop. It would be easier to tell if the damn sign would stop *moving*. Trying — and failing — to read the bus schedule, eventually my eyes shut, because what's the point in leaving them open?

I don't remember sitting down — or collapsing, more likely — but now I'm on the ground. My body is, anyway; the rest of me floats in dizzying darkness. It doesn't matter when the bus is supposed to come, because I'll be waiting either way; waiting to get on, then waiting to get off; and once I get home, I'll be waiting in my apartment — waiting, as always, to live, to die.

What does it matter *where* the waiting happens?

All I know is, I can't keep walking, can hardly even look up when I hear a voice I don't recognize:

"Hey, you're pathetic, you know that?"

My yawning eyes discover, towering over me, the blurry shape of someone reaching down, as if to help me. But what she says next is about as helpful as a blow to the gut: "Are you seriously such a wimp that you can't stand up? God, what a waste of lungs."

Run away! Run! But the best I can do is recoil into despair.

Because I'm utterly aware, without being reminded, how pathetic I am; the pain ropes me back a few years, back to that fateful day when the Fog was unleashed, and I just happened to be at the epicenter of the contamination zone . . .

My thoughts disperse at the harsh squeal of brakes, followed by the rumble of an idling engine and the hiss of shuttle doors — none of which is nearly as obnoxious as what comes next:

"Snap out of it, loser. Aren't you getting on the bus? Can't you even manage that?"

Peering out from the void of my memories, it takes me a second to realize I've accepted the stranger's hand, allowing her to help me up. Coughing through noxious puffs of diesel exhaust, I take one step, trip, and fall again. Soon I'm practically getting carried — wounded soldier-style — onto the bus. The air around me buzzes with concerned tones, but the palpable worry in every voice doesn't take the edge off what's being said, even if I'm the only one hearing it:

"Keep holding onto me, unless you're as weak as you look."

"Ah, stop wasting your time and just drop that piece of crap!"

I notice the bus driver staring expectantly at me, eyebrows raised halfway to the ceiling. "Ah great," he says from behind the oversized steering wheel, "here comes another heap of street trash smelling up my bus. No free rides, you know." He taps the payment machine.

Digging in my pocket, it dawns on me that I left my wallet at home.

The laugh arrives unbidden — an ugly bark flying up my throat.

"What's so funny?" the driver asks.

The only response I can muster is another terrible laugh, and another. *Wouldn't have even been able to buy that bag of chips.* Pretty soon I'm sobbing hysterically.

"I'll pay for their fare," says the woman who carried me.

Across the bus, others chime in:

"It isn't worth it!"

"They'll be dead before they can repay you!"

"Why are you wasting time helping someone who can't help themself?"

That's the last stab through my ears before I disentangle myself from my savior and turn around. I'm still cracking up as I stumble off the bus, back onto the street. Somehow I'll make it home. Even — especially — if it kills me.

Maybe it's my imagination, but I think someone's getting off the bus behind me, hurling another slew of existential insults in my direction; or is it just wishful thinking, to hope for some company, even as I'm walking away, because being stepped on is still better than being alone?

Because being hurt is still some type of . . . *being*.

In any case, I must have been hallucinating; the next time I crumple to the ground, there's nobody reaching down to help me up.

Either I'm seeing double or I now have two psychiatric contagion specialists working my case.

The room at the clinic is small, bright, very white, and quiet compared to the hospital which had discharged me yesterday. But beneath that precious lack of noise, the phantom beep of a heart-monitor still grows in my ears, planted deep in my mind, watered and given light by the hospital staff over the past few nights (or was it decades, centuries?) as they hooked me up and plugged me in, and poked and prodded me with instruments I don't dare to mention, for fear of remembering.

Yet no instrument is more scarring in the depths of its range than the human voice.

"Aren't you even capable of answering me?" asks my psychiatrist(s). His image blurs; there are suddenly two of him, then one again, depending on how hard I stare. However many healthcare providers are really sitting across from me, they speak with one voice: "You're making a horrible mistake by refusing to talk to me. Nobody is going to help you unless you allow yourself to be helped . . ."

My attention drifts to an empty chair in the corner. I'd love to just sink into that chair and let the world dissolve around me. But in this place, I am required to sit on this bed which is not a bed, crinkling its paper sheet beneath my twitching haunches.

"Hello? Are you hearing me? Or are your ears as weak as your will to live?"

Clearing my throat, I take some meager refuge in that personal realm of darkness behind my eyelids. "Yes, I can hear you. And I'm well aware of how weak I am. I've known for some time, thank you."

When I open my eyes, I find that my reply is met with a strange look of pity — an expression, perhaps, intended to remind me that whatever I say still turns out to be . . . well, exactly what I've said, regardless of how the words of others change when they hit me. As in, essentially I've responded to something which wasn't said, referencing something — my weakness — which wasn't actually brought up . . . except through the Fog.

The specialist crosses his legs in an admirable attempt to hide his impatience. "Hey, this isn't an attack, okay? You're not the victim of anyone but yourself."

He's trying to help, like they were at the hospital . . . like they claimed to be . . . But I can't stop what's already coming out of my mouth: "That's not true. You're hurting me. Always, all of you, everyone."

A subdued sigh. "Come on, we've been over this. Nobody is asking you to do the impossible. There are plenty of people who've contracted the Fog, but unlike you, they learn to manage it and get along with society. The question is, when are *you* going to learn?"

The double vision is starting to make me feel ganged up on. "I don't want to be here anymore. Can I go now? Is the appointment over?"

My psychiatrist — my nemesis — puts on a smile that never reaches his eyes. "Please, I need you to help me understand. Help me understand why precious resources were wasted to save your life when the paramedics found you passed out on the sidewalk."

I possess no answer; I'm shutting down, zippering myself into the pocket universe in the back of my brain, where I may not be at peace but at least I am at home. Thanks to various intravenous drips, I am less exhausted, less dehydrated, and less malnourished than I was before the ambulance picked me up — before those nights spent in the kind of hell where you end up after *not* jumping off a bridge. But I'm still empty on the inside, still hungry in a different way, still tired in the *only* way . . . Empty, yes, hollowed-out — yet somehow carrying too much, always too much. How does anybody hold all of these memories, these emotions? How is it physically possible for a human to carry such weight for a lifetime?

I'm thinking about jumping off bridges again when I say, "I have no idea how I'm going to afford that ambulance ride."

"You could cry about it. I'm sure that would help."

The bed-paper crumples and rips under my restless legs.

"For all I know," the psychiatrist continues, polite as you like, "you're just doing this for attention. You realize that's the only reason anyone ever commits suicide, right? To make waves . . ."

The river calls to me again, glowing in my imagination like the exit sign above a door. I can hardly contain the urge to run, just run until I hit the flashing water . . .

"You're not the first person to try to starve yourself," he says. "If you hate yourself so much, why are you still hanging around with the living? Oh . . . I see now." This psychiatric contagion specialist — this man who knows everything — leans closer. And for one among many spiraling moments, I am convinced, honest-to-God convinced, that what he's saying is what he's actually saying. "You're making a political statement, is that it? Don't tell me you're one of those conspiracy theorists who believes the Fog wasn't an accident." His deep-seated opinion begins to shine through, too impassioned to be corrupted by my affliction; indeed, he must be speaking directly from the heart, the sole organ where such sure-footed indignation can spawn. "The government didn't do this to you, got it? You're not the victim of some top-secret biological attack. You're only the victim of yourself."

I nod along, bobbing my head to take the edge off his intensity. "I understand—"

"I don't think you do. Yes, the Fog was a psycho-biological contaminant developed by military scientists. Yes, it was created to disrupt enemy communications on the ground and cause chaos in hostile regions." His pause, punctuated with a long, weary sigh, carries all the condescension of a teacher who's given up and doesn't see the use of scolding the student, but must get through the lesson nonetheless. "Still, there's no evidence — absolutely none — that our government purposefully released the Fog on our own population as a test, like nutcases such as yourself tend to insist."

At this point my fists are full of the bed-paper, balling and tearing. Trying to focus on the sensation, the feel of the material . . . cheap and easily ripped, a cross between toilet paper and butcher paper. The kind of paper you'd use to wipe excrement or wrap dead meat — or, apparently, to sit on, to make an uncomfortable experience more uncomfortable.

"I need to go," I say. "I'm leaving."

It's like this guy doesn't hear me. "Our country wouldn't do something like that — unleash a biohazard on its own people." He laughs easily, naturally, the way other people laugh, the way I've given up on. "Don't tell me you're scared the government is watching you. Spying on your symptoms, keeping tabs on their experiment . . ."

I'm out the door by that time — but I'm not running, not screaming, because I don't want to give anyone a reason to bring me back here, not ever again.

Outside the clinic a stone pillar catches me, supporting my

body, if not the rest of me. What street is this? Squinting against the bite of the sun, I can't see anything familiar. Can't see . . . the point. I begin to slide down . . .

She finds me basically how she found me the first time: curled up on the sidewalk, dying relatively slowly, but only relatively. A bug baking on the pavement. Vision hazy, I don't really recognize her until she reaches to help me, like she helped me at that bus stop days ago. So it's not like she's just some angel manifesting whole-cloth into my life in my darkest hour; rather, she's been here a while, hidden without hiding.

In the nicest tone possible, she delivers her greeting: "Oh, not you again. God, don't you ever give up on being pathetic?"

I'm crawling away. "Please," I tell her, this angel or demon, "I don't want to suffer anymore." I'm causing a scene — passersby are stopping, gathering around — but I don't care. I've never cared — never. *If only that were true.* I am what I am; I am nothing, surrounded by everything; but I'm not distracted, no; I'm solely concentrated on not hurting. And I'm saying, "Don't you think I can see how pathetic I am? Look at me! I don't need reminding!"

"I wasn't saying . . ." She stops, suddenly getting it. "You were hit by the Fog, weren't you?" She smiles a sad, hoping smile. "Listen, I'm not trying to hurt you."

Those words glance off me, and it requires every muscle I don't have, every muscle nobody has, in order to pull the meaning back, to understand that, for once, I'm capable of . . . understanding. "Did you just say . . ."

She's practically beaming. "You heard me right."

"How?" My legs plant themselves solidly beneath me, raising me up. "The Fog makes it impossible for me to interpret . . ." But a fiercely entrenched instinct holds back the rest of that sentence. Too many times have I brought up my diagnosis only to be labeled a victim or a monster. *What's the difference between the two anyway?* I'd rather one less person despises me, especially the first person in years I've been able to actually understand.

"I can explain later why my words aren't being corrupted by your condition," she says with extraordinary calm. "For now, let's get you a meal. You look like a skeleton."

That almost knocks me back down. Luckily she grabs me, this stranger; she keeps me stable, somehow not just physically.

She says — she really says, "Sorry." And it sounds like she might even mean it. "Shouldn't have called you a skeleton. But seriously, dude, you must be starving."

"I can't eat. You don't understand."

"Correct me if I'm wrong, but if you've got the Fog, isn't not understanding *your* problem?"

My cheeks are wet. When did I start crying? *Better question — how did I ever stop?* The bridge sits heavy in my mind; the river plays against my memory, a shining, self-prescribed death sentence.

I tell this woman what I wish I could have told my psychiatrist. "I'm not worth saving. I've made too many mistakes."

"You couldn't have made that many mistakes, because here you are, alive. That's proof you've done all right."

I am stunned. There's simply no other word. Which is why, I suppose, I tag along to the nearest diner without putting up a fight. Stumbling toward something edible, following my new friend, wondering why she cares.

"It's called Clarity," she says through a mouthful of eggs and bacon. "Clarity with a capital 'C.'"

I'm stirring a second packet of fake sugar into my steaming decaf. Haven't touched the food yet, though she ordered enough breakfast for both of us. "Clarity. Is that the brand-name for a new antidepressant or something?"

"Pharmaceuticals can be part of it, but no, Clarity isn't just drugs."

I lean back, pushing against the stiff cushions of the booth, not sipping my coffee, not relaxing. The diner reeks of the casually forgotten: crusty syrup and ketchup bottles that haven't been cleaned in years, much less refrigerated, are bookended by near-empty salt and pepper shakers; ancient shoe-crud cakes the linoleum floor, too far gone to be removed, just like the age-old gum stuck under our table. Yet the morning — or is it afternoon now? — bleeds brightly through grease-smudged windows, making the restaurant glow in its own filthy way, while making me squint. Despite my half-closed eyes, it's difficult not to notice how the surrounding tables, and even our server, can't stop staring at me. I must truly look like a monster. And I'll bet I smell like one too. The only person who doesn't seem repulsed by me is the woman who brought me here, if her humongous appetite is any indication. So I ask, "How are you able . . . or how am *I* able . . ."

"To hear what I'm really saying?" She shovels a mound of hashbrowns. "Let's back up. My name is Serena. Doctor Serena Baile."

I cross my arms, giving her nothing, not even a look.

She — this self-styled Doctor Serena — says, "It's okay if you don't want to tell me your name."

My anger flashes. "It's okay if you don't want to tell me what you're a doctor of."

Serena snorts, almost chokes. "Touché." She begins methodically dissecting an omelet with her fork. "I'm a . . . well, an unusual kind of doctor. Maybe we can leave it at that. Also, aren't you going to eat anything?"

"Food tastes like chalk these days."

"Have you ever actually eaten chalk?"

"No." Though I wouldn't be surprised if *she* has, given the rate at which she's currently devouring everything in front of her. "That doesn't mean—"

Doctor Serena pushes a tower of flapjacks under my nose. "Trust me, these pancakes don't taste like anything except *good*."

My gaze dips down, grudgingly checking out the flat brown

sponges piled high atop the plate. "Why are you trying so hard to help me?"

She offers an expression I can only describe as . . . comfortable. Like maybe she's one of those rare souls who appears on the outside to be the same person she inhabits on the inside; that is, this Doctor Serena Baile is quite possibly capable of looking at herself in mirrors, and it shows. She says, "I would have followed you last time, tried to help more. But I didn't want to . . . you know, follow you. It seemed like you wanted to be on your own. I guess I should have figured you were suffering from—"

"What do you know about suffering?" I don't care that my voice is rising. I don't care that the people sitting across the restaurant are sharing looks that are meant to be seen. "You haven't helped me yet, *doctor*. Not one iota."

"Oh, I didn't bring you here to help you. This is all about helping myself, in fact. It's part of my Clarity regimen."

"So you're projecting your problems onto me?"

"Not quite. I'm simply living — and dying — the way I want to."

This catches me off-guard. I take a cold sip of coffee and wait. But Serena seems determined to make me press, and eventually I buckle. "Explain what Clarity is, then."

She shrugs, like this isn't the first time in years that I've talked, really talked, to someone. "Drugs and therapy are pieces of the puzzle. But Clarity is larger than those things. It's the willingness to listen, to learn, to study and admire, when your former self might have only . . . blankly witnessed. And — ah, I can tell I'm losing you."

"Not losing — already lost."

She chuckles like I made a joke. "Clarity is difficult to put into words. It's different for everyone. I have certain needs, for instance, but nobody else has the same needs as me. The best way to put it is . . . well, Clarity comes from inside you."

I suppress the overwhelming urge to shout. "But how? How am I hearing what you're saying without getting hurt?"

"Whether you realize it or not, we've entered into an unspoken pact. Call it *mutual respect*, or whatever you want, but since the second time I found you, we've begun to see one another clearly. I suspect what happened was this: for whatever reason, we engaged with each other in a completely different manner than you've ever engaged with anyone since the Fog—"

"You *suspect*?"

"Just because I'm a doctor doesn't mean I know everything." She drizzles the pancakes with syrup. "I know what Clarity is for me, and that's all. Ironically I think the fact that I'm *not* trying to tell you how to live your life is possibly what's allowing you to hear what I *am* telling you."

Confused and exhausted, my head droops.

"You don't sleep much, do you?"

"I can't submit myself to the past like that."

"Then you do care about yourself."

"You still haven't given me any answers."

"Not having answers for you *is* an answer." Meanwhile she hasn't stopped drenching her pancakes. "The only answers you need are going to come from you, not me," she says, sticking one dripping chunk of pancake into her mouth, then another, and *another*. It's as if her appetite cannot be contained by mere food. "Your pain has no effect on me. Doesn't make me upset or frustrated or even sad. Everything I'm doing for you, I'm doing for myself, in the healthiest way. Likewise, nothing I'm saying can be adulterated by the Fog, because — here's where I'm speculating — at the moment, you aren't getting triggered by someone attempting to influence you. That's what I hope, at least. Because you're stronger than you believe. You're proving it with every second you don't walk away. And that's not validation. That's simply an observation."

In a dream-like daze, I'm watching her tear into her second pancake as if she's never eaten a full meal in her life. "How can you talk about what's 'healthy' when you're inhaling cakes soaked in sugar and butter? Maybe you're not jumping off a bridge, but you're still killing yourself, just at a slower pace."

Doctor Serena puts on a silly frown. "Remember what I said about Clarity being different for everyone? Well, food is part of my personal recipe for happiness — especially butter and sugar. A lot of butter, and a lot of sugar. Not too much. Just a lot."

"You're claiming what's bad for one person might be good for someone else. But some things are just bad. The Fog, for instance, isn't good for anyone. And . . ." I catch myself, but then decide to say it anyway. "And suicidal thoughts aren't good for anyone."

"Beg to differ, pal." She's on her third pancake and showing no sign of slowing down. "You're going to have a much better idea of what you need out of life after you're done wishing you were dead."

"What do you know about my pain?"

"Pain doesn't belong to you exclusively. You think others haven't gone through the ringer? There's only one difference that matters between your pain and my pain: that you believe there's a difference."

It requires every rational bone in my body not to throw my coffee at the wall and storm away. Rage doesn't begin to describe it. This is . . . this is *hatred*. "The Fog must be twisting your words again, because I could have sworn you just assumed your pain is the same as my pain. But from looking at you, it's pretty clear you're not dealing with the pain I'm dealing with."

"Now who's doing the assuming?" Serena polishes off the last pancake in record time, and returns to devouring her omelet without skipping a beat. "Your pain, similar to your anger right now, is a disease which doesn't want you to think you've got a disease. The thing is, the pain won't allow you to connect with others until you realize that the pain isn't yours alone. The pain belongs to all of us. The pain *feeds* off of the belief that nobody knows how you feel . . . But even if that were true, the pain can be of service to you once you stop hurting alone."

"Is there any other way to hurt?"

She smiles again. "We all burn under the same sun, just at different times, and at different temperatures. Maybe it's bright for someone else when it's night for you. That doesn't mean your day won't come."

The coffee buzzes my head even though it's decaf. "What if the pain never goes away, though?"

"That sounds like a framing issue. We aren't supposed to get *rid* of the pain, not all of it. That's the beauty of pain — it's an asset, a guide. The pain itself is what helps you get through . . . the pain."

"What does that even mean?"

At long last she stops eating, puts down her fork, and folds her sticky hands business-like on the table. "It might seem like a betrayal — to yourself, and others — to say that pain can cause happiness, that pain facilitates a deeper Clarity — deeper caring, deeper wonder. But it's true: pain shows us what is precious. Pain is something to be *thankful* for. Even if it weren't — even if there was nothing beneficial about pain — nobody who's in pain can afford to think that way! The pain *wants* you to fight against it. That's how the pain wins. But if we *learn* from it instead of resisting it, eventually we graduate from the lesson. And if we know pain, we know each other."

"You don't know me."

"On the contrary, you've been allowing me to get to know you for a while now. Thank you for that." She cracks her neck, then her knuckles, then her back. "You see, at this point in time, we're connecting. And connection doesn't happen alone. The only way you can connect is *together*."

"People don't connect with me. They only hurt me."

"Sure, others can hurt you on the outside; that's up to them. But only you can hurt yourself on the inside." She points at me with her eyes — points directly at me with wide brown eyes. "Yes, you can be made a victim. But you can never be made to *embrace* your victimhood."

"That's the most condescending thing I've ever heard."

"I don't think so. Or else you wouldn't have heard it."

"I want to go home now." But her eyes have caught me, trapped me, and I can't bring myself to get up.

"You're already home," she explains with her strange happy-sadness. "There is a limitless, beautiful world which will always be yours, and only yours. That world exists on the inside, not the outside. Unfortunately, like any good home, this one requires you to build it and maintain it. Which takes some serious strength. A lot more strength than it takes to build those other things we call 'homes,' but are really just houses."

I don't remember finishing my coffee, but now my hands are wrapped around an empty mug, and my heart raps a nervous rhythm. "Okay, you might be strong, but that doesn't mean I am. So don't hold your strength over me."

She laughs. "We can't hold strength over each other. But if we aren't careful, we can forever hold onto lies — because those flimsy things weigh practically nothing, and are dangerously easy to carry."

I shake my head. "You're giving me vertigo."

"Time for me to go, then." She slides out of the booth, brushing food off her shirt. "Besides, this conversation isn't helping me anymore."

"Just like that?"

She pulls out some cash and sticks it under a plate, plenty to cover the bill and leave a generous tip. "I'm confident you'll be all right without me. You're a survivor."

"How can you be sure?"

"Because here you are."

"You still haven't told me what you're a doctor of."

"You still haven't told me your name."

Is that an offer? An invite? But even if I wanted to give her my name, at this rate, what would I say? When your name feels like the last remaining piece of you, is it really anyone's name at all?

Serena blinks — or is that a wink? "That's okay. There's always next time to introduce yourself."

"Next time?"

"Say, Monday at noon? Same place?" Without giving me room to say no, she turns to leave. And before I can think of what I'll later wish to have called after her, she's gone.

I follow Doctor Serena Baile, not with my legs, but with my eyes; I follow her through the smudged window, through the brightness beyond, until she disappears around the street corner. I wonder if I'll ever see her again. It's a choice I haven't made yet.

The window is covered in greasy fingerprints. It looks like some kid was trying to draw or write on the glass. A hungry message from the past, reminding me of that other message, the one written on the bridge:

If you're reading this . . .

Suddenly the weather turns, and it's pouring outside. How quickly everything can change, I think. How terribly, wonderfully quick.

I want to be upset that the strange doctor left so abruptly. I *want* . . . to be hurt. But it strikes me, as the rain strikes the window, that she left because she didn't pity me. She left because she was no longer getting anything out of our exchange.

Which means, before she left — somehow, in some way — I really must have been helping her. Something I haven't done in years.

To . . . help.

Huddled in my booth, facing the darkening day, I'm grinning. (The expression crept up on me.) I'm not buying that zen crap Serena tried selling me: pain can't always be good for you — it just can't be. There must be a level of misery at which point the only answer is to escape . . . that is, to jump . . .

But have I honestly reached that level?

Or am I just afraid to reach inside myself?

The server hasn't cleared the plates yet, and there's still some hashbrowns left. It's barely a conscious decision when I grab my fork and wolf down those cold, ketchup-stained potatoes, because I'm too caught up thinking: *Afraid to reach inside . . .* Yes, the key is fear. Or, the *locked door* is fear, and the key is something more like . . .

My gut growls. I'm beginning to feel sick. Sickened. I push away the food, but too late — a cramp spreads through my intestines. A sharp, expanding worm. But that pain . . . well, it's almost nice. Nice to feel sick. A signal, loud and clear. An answer, or a hint of one, coming from within.

A . . . clarity.

Now: the sensation of being watched. I glance around. Have I seen that man before — that man who just sat down? Is he a government agent, following me to collect data on the effects of the Fog? Was Doctor Serena Baile also a spy? (*She never did tell me what she was a doctor of . . .*) Am I some sort of guinea pig in a massive bio-weapon experiment?

But the wave of paranoia crashes, and passes, and I'm left with the old, original fear of nothing too specific, of existence itself. Left with the urge to run back to that bridge and fall from it like the rain . . . but ironically, it's fear which has kept me from doing that, I believe. The only reason I'm still alive — here's the truth — is because I'm even more scared to die.

I want to cry and cry. I really *want* to. But I'd have to force the tears out. I simply don't have the energy. It's not a reflex, to cry, but a craving, one I'm afraid to indulge. There's the fear again . . . but these cheeks don't need to be watered anymore, because there's nothing growing on my face except a smile.

I wish I'd told the doctor my name. But this way I've got something to look forward to.

The rain is getting worse. People are hurrying inside from the street. A mob of soaked and miserable souls. With everyone in the world cramming themselves into this diner, I've never had a greater urge to get out, to run and scream. Despite my hurry to remove myself from the dryness, the loudness, the crowded room,

I can't get through the doorway. Too many people, a horde, pushing and desperate. Before I know it, I'm holding the door, helping them all get inside, simply so that I can get *outside*.

But regardless of my intentions, I am . . . helping.

The door is good to hold, unlike so many things I've held for so long. I keep holding it, that door, welcoming the rush of wet bodies blowing past me. And it occurs to me, in this moment, on this day, that I could do anything, absolutely anything, that I want to do. Nobody is stopping me.

The door is wide open.

I could head for the bridge. But there's another option: I could head home, and pick up some food on the way. Maybe a can of spray paint too. Assuming the weather clears up, which isn't much of an assumption.

Eventually, inevitably, the weather always does.

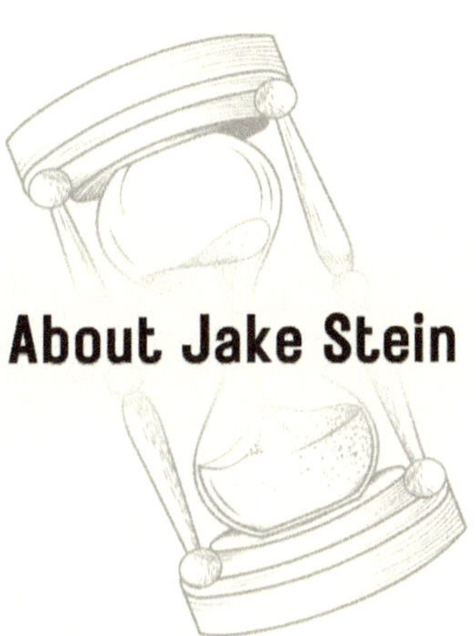

About Jake Stein

Jake Stein survives despite all odds in Portland, OR, where he concocts strange tales on his laptop and spends too much time at Powell's Books. His work has appeared or is forthcoming in Lightspeed Magazine, Ellery Queen Mystery Magazine, and Aurealis. You can occasionally find him stumbling around Bluesky @jakeiswriting.bsky.social or Twitter @jakewritesagain

The Lucky One

by H.M. Joinville

MIRANDA WAKES up at 3:30 am every morning to the muffled screams from upstairs. On a usual day, she would go into the kitchen, grab a bottle of water and some crackers, and sit in the window to watch the stars glistening above the tops of the darkened buildings.

Today, however, when she shuffles into the kitchen in her worn house slippers, she finds she is out of crackers and down to her last three bottles of Evian. A single can of low-sodium black beans stares back at her from the upper cabinet.

She takes one of the bottles, pours it slowly into her small metal cooking pot, and lights the camp stove. She watches as tiny bubbles rise to the surface. Pouring herself a mug, she brings the steaming liquid to her lips and sips. A familiar warmth fills her chest. The weather is turning cold, and the chill seeps into every crack of her pre-war apartment in Queens.

Taking her mug, she sits in her father's favorite chair. She still remembers when he brought it home. A curbside discount he had called it, his voice filled with pride. Her mother had cursed under her breath, thrown her hands up, and left the room. It had a worn yellow spot in the otherwise brown pleather seat and cat scratches down the back, but he loved it.

She takes out her sketchpad and lets it sit unopened on her lap.

"Miranda," her father once told her, "you have it in you to draw right down to the soul of a person. That's a gift. You're lucky. Most people float through life never knowing why they're even here."

He had bought her the sketchpad last fall, before she intended to start college and study art. She wonders how many students are still walking around the campus.

On the end table sits a bottle of pills, her mug, and a candle she picked up at Target last week that smells too much like laundry soap.

Today is the day, she thinks to herself, unscrewing the top. She tips her head back as the pills fill the pockets of her cheeks. Just swallow. Do it. The inside of her mouth tastes metallic and bitter. She breathes in through her nose as her gag reflex activates. Rushing to the bathroom, she spits them out into the sink. Their tiny white bodies clamor around the porcelain. Another scream comes from upstairs.

"Shut up! Just shut the fuck up and die already!"

Her knees hit the cold tile floor with an impact that radiates up to her teeth. She cups her hands over her ears and squeezes her eyes closed.

Without knowing why, except for the growing desire to join in the horrible chorus, she begins to scream along, as loud as her lungs will allow, until her throat is raw and her voice softens to a whimper.

"I'm lucky. I'm lucky," she repeats as a mantra or a prayer until her breathing slows and her shoulders slump forward in resignation.

Wiping the snot running down her upper lip with the sleeve

of her sweatshirt, she returns to her sketchpad. She thinks back, trying to remember every detail of her last subject, sketching in the shadows and lines of a face. The curve of the nose and the set of the jaw. She stops to examine the arch of her back, bent over in pain. The eyes are wide, reflecting a mix of surprise and terror. It's a young woman in her early to mid-twenties — about her age.

She writes at the bottom, "Journal entry #136." She flips the page over and continues her documentation.

Location: 82nd Street in the apartment above the old arcade.

Clothing: Jeans, Nirvana t-shirt, and black Converse.

A small smile slowly spreads across her lips. If things had been different, she would have liked this woman. Her sketchpad is filled cover to cover with similarly tortured faces.

Finally, she scribbles down:

Type: Cycle.

From her experience, she has learned that there exist three outcomes to what happened after the attack. There aren't any news cycles or late-night talking heads in the apocalypse; FEMA didn't swoop in with their tents, aid workers didn't bring her a shiny blanket, and radio calls went unanswered. So she doesn't know all the details. She studies what remains, though, like a case worker in Hell. Being the last person left alive, she considers herself the leading expert.

#1. You die, and you follow the bright light into whatever version of the afterlife you subscribe to (like her father).

This type accounts for about 20%* of the population. *All statistics are made-up because they really don't matter anymore, do they? She spent a solid week retracing every possible route between their apartment and the hospital to confirm he was gone. It was her only comfort.

#2. You die, but your soul, or ghost, or spirit, sticks around and relives an infinite cycle of your own death. (AKA: the closest thing she has seen to Hell.) This group makes up about 75%*, or what she calls the unlucky majority. Most of the time, people repeat the same tasks, day after fucking day. That is, until the end of their loop, when the shit hits the fan. She avoids this scene at all costs.

There are always some assholes in the lot and at roughly 4.9%* of the remaining population and taking up 90%** of the fucks she has left to give, **verified statistic, we have . . .

#3. You die, and you come back, but as something else. Not a ghost, but an energy that has no purpose, just a ball of white-hot fuck you. It can take any form, possess any power, and generally be the worst goddamn grab bag you will ever encounter.

Why this happens to certain people can only be speculated upon. Maybe it was something buried in their DNA, or maybe they were just assholes when they were alive, too. Thus, proving that while the world can end, not everything, in fact, changes. Running across a Cat:3, as she likes to call them, is a day-ruiner.

One could light up an entire city block at night. Flames erupt from its charred skin, and smoke pours from it like an inky black waterfall that burn her eyes and fill her nose with a putrid odor.

Another could send out a wave of energy, like a bolt of lightning. One had come crashing down so powerfully that it knocked her out for half a day. She still gets antsy at the sight of storm clouds.

Turning the page, a photograph slips free and floats to the ground. Landing face up, she sees in the flicker of candlelight, ghosts of a past life she has almost forgotten.

In it, she couldn't be older than ten, and her mother and father look so much younger than she ever remembers them being. They are all smiling and wearing their hiking gear. Her mother clutches a trekking pole triumphantly above her head, and Miranda has her arms wrapped around her father's waist. They had regularly taken trips like this upstate when she was young, before her mother got sick. A ball grows in the base of her throat at the memory of that happiness and how fleeting it was.

There is a fourth outcome. She is the fourth outcome.

#4. You live

Another scream echoes, this time from down the hall. There is one other thing she recalls about those trips — silence. There were birds and animals and the wind blowing through the trees, but otherwise there was pure silence. She goes to the closet and pulls out the small camping tent they kept after her mother's death. They had begun talking about taking another trip as recently as last summer.

It would take at least three or four days, maybe more, to get there. She knows her way around the city no problem, but once she gets north of the Bronx, she'll need a map.

In a worn backpack, she packs the can of beans, water, a half-full can of neon pink spray paint, a few clean pairs of socks and underwear, a pair of jeans, her favorite hoodie, and her art supplies. After a momentary pause, she goes into her father's bedroom. It feels odd to just walk in, so she gives the door a customary knock, which is met by silence. His clothes are still scattered on the floor.

She approaches his unmade bed and pulls out a large lock box from under it. It's a number combo — her birthday. A large-caliber revolver, which he bought for himself on his 50th birth-day, and a round of ammunition rest inside. He always wanted to be a cowboy, Miranda thinks as she picks it up. It's heavier than she imagined. The cold metal glistens in the morning sunlight. She finds the holster in his top drawer, puts it on, and looks at herself in the mirror.

"Let's get the fuck out of Dodge."

Before she leaves, she grabs her noise-canceling headphones off the kitchen table — they're the must-have accessory for the fall of humanity — and loops them around her neck as she steps out of the apartment one final time.

Ms. Rivera comes up the stairs just as she does dozens of times each day. Her form is nearly translucent as she struggles with two large paper bags of groceries and another canvas tote slung under her left arm. At seventy, it's a wonder she was able to manage the three flights to their floor when she was alive.

"I'm sorry I never helped you," she wants to tell her, but instead she only says, "Bye, Ms. Rivera," over her shoulder, not waiting for the reply. She pauses momentarily at the sound of . . . a gasp? No, only the sound of a door closing.

She grabs a few protein bars and a sports drink at the bodega on her street. She can grab more along the way.

She spends the morning as usual, sitting on a park bench like when she was young, creating elaborate backstories for anyone who passes by. It was their game, hers and her father's. They would eat their lunches and call it "Dine and Dish."

Now she does it alone with her sketchpad and pencils, feverishly trying to memorialize them all. As if remembering even false lives is better than being forgotten entirely.

"Veronica," she says to no one as the misty outline of a woman walks by in tight leggings, talking through a headset and pushing a baby in a stroller. Their shimmering forms are like early morning fog, their movements almost dream-like.

"An advertising executive. My guess is she is out on maternity leave, enjoys vodka sodas and trendy pop-ups, and has 2 million followers on Instagram."

When she turns to her left, she half-expects to see her father there, ready to jump in with a joke about how the baby's name is Clover Fields, Piston Engine, or something else just as ridiculous.

Veronica stops to fiddle with the blanket in the stroller and coo at the baby inside.

"No, it's Emilia," Miranda says with a catch in her throat.

"She would have grown up to be a dental hygienist, married her college sweetheart, Tony, and honeymooned in Barcelona."

"Hey, Ronnie!" Miranda calls out. "Want to grab a drink later and catch up? Great! I'll call you. Get a babysitter."

Without acknowledging her presence, Veronica stands, discreetly adjusts her sports bra, and walks away.

As the sun begins to dip in the sky, Miranda finds a park and sets up her tent. She pulls the beans from her pack and eats them, grimacing as the cold mush slides down her throat. She's too tired to attempt a fire. Outside, the chattering of voices fills the air; a baby cries, and a dog barks.

If she doesn't see them, she can almost imagine that the world is as it was before. She tries to make out bits of conversation. What was it we talked about back then? It feels like a lifetime ago. What worries kept us up at night?

The crowd grows restless, as if they know what is about to happen, like animals sensing danger. Sighing, Miranda pulls on her headphones and closes her eyes. The slight buzz of silence steadies her nerves as the tent begins to shake violently. A scream pierces through.

After the tent settles, she reaches over, unzips the flap, and pulls it back. The park is empty. The ground, once pristine, is littered with garbage and heaps of clothes.

With a flicker you would expect to see on a faded 1950s television set, dozens of people slowly begin to return. The talking commences as if nothing has occurred. An elderly woman walks her dog, two teen girls chat on a blanket on the grass, and a couple sit arm in arm on the edge of the fountain.

"I'm lucky. I'm lucky," Miranda repeats to herself until she falls asleep.

In the morning, clouds hang low and dark, making her feel almost claustrophobic even on the empty streets, with high-rises towering on both sides, a canyon of abandoned stores and office space. A booming sound of overturned trash cans and broken windows emerges from around the corner. She sucks in her breath at the sight. Meandering into her path comes a large grizzly bear, a femur clutched between its teeth, likely an escapee from the Central Park Zoo.

"Good girl," she says, lowering her eyes, as a low huff rumbles from its throat. She reaches for the gun as the beast barrels towards her.

"Shit, shit, shit," she curses. Aims. Fires. Everything slows down. She can hear her rapid breathing and her heart pounding. She watches as the bullet pierces the bear's left eye and explodes. Propelled by force, the animal slams into her, knocking her to the ground. Her body crumples at the impact. Her headphones fly off, and she follows, dragging herself beneath the belly of a Kia Forte.

Loud banging and the sounds of crunching metal wash over her. The car shakes above her. When the bear's blood-soaked muzzle pokes under, looking for a stray limb to grab ahold of, she fires again. This time, she takes her time. The shot frees its jaw like a loose hinge, swinging with every movement. The bear wipes at its mangled face with its paws and, with a cry of anger and pain, flees around the corner, a trail of blood in its wake.

Sliding out, she assesses her body for injuries. Her hands tremble with the rush of adrenaline pumping through her veins. Her ankle is sore, likely twisted or sprained. Her head is bleeding from a gash across her forehead. Head wounds are real gushers. Otherwise, she's in one piece.

Bending down, she pulls the headphones free from their hiding place under the Kia. They are split down the middle, and one side hangs by a single wire. Worthless. She drops them into the nearest trash can.

A mile down the road, against the side of a shoe store, a mural displays a man's head with a globe tattooed across his scalp. He holds his face in his hands. The words "The world wept" are written beneath. Miranda stops, pulls out the can of spray paint, and shakes it.

There is a moment of admiration before she aims and writes, "Still Here." Then, as an afterthought, marks through the word "wept" and replaces it with "died."

At the sight of a grocery store, her stomach growls. She needs more supplies and bandages. Next door, a sign reads Parking - 1

Hour $20, more than minimum wage. Even now, she can't hide her disgust. A cemetery with license plates as tombstones. Half-sticking out of the entrance, mid-merge, is a red Tesla. Its windows are blown out.

The driver sits behind the wheel, patches of tissue still clinging to his skeletal frame; a bird's nest, with bits of dried grass, discarded plastic straws, and white downy feathers fill his gaping mouth. One of his arms rests in the open window. The other one hangs limp at his side.

"Hey, dude, watch my stuff, will ya?" she asks as she deposits her tent in the backseat. One less thing to carry around for a while. The jostling of the vehicle sends his head forward and into his lap.

The grocery store shelves still contain tidy rows of food. If people had been warned, if they had known it was the end, they would have stripped the place bare, as if toilet paper and flat screens would've saved them.

Next to the door, an ancient metal newsstand still displays the final headline pressed against the glass, "Nuclear Deal Reached." Miranda has read this article.

She had worked the night shift and gotten up late. It was long after her father had gone to the hospital for his chemo. He never wanted to bother her with his treatments and opted for a cab if it meant waking her.

The newspaper lay across the kitchen table in a disheveled pile. She popped some bread in the toaster and went searching for the arts and leisure section. A friend, Sied, was about to open a new gallery. The headline had grabbed her attention.

She had read the article twice. While it parroted all the right talking points, one important detail it didn't address — one that became everything. The President had reached a nuclear deal, but he and half of Congress ignored reports from their own intelligence agencies of more dangerous biological weapons being tested. There were rumors on Reddit boards and social media, and leaks to the independent press, but nothing had stopped the attack.

Miranda touches the sharp metal corner as she walks by, hoping she can somehow reach back into the past. The store smells of rotting meat from the deli, thawed dinners in the freezer section, and the bodies. The crunch of a hand beneath her foot causes vomit to rise in the back of her throat.

She goes for the essentials first: toilet paper, jerky, two more cans of beans, and trail mix. As she pulls a sports drink from its plastic ring, the squeaking of a rusty front wheel pierces the silence. A flicker, and the aisles are jam-packed with phantom shoppers filling their carts.

It's only a matter of time now. Her ankle throbs in her boot. She needs to find bandages and painkillers fast.

"Oof, sorry," she begins, absentmindedly as she turns, and nearly collides with the foggy outline of a worker stocking the shelves with boxes of pasta.

In his mid-thirties, the man's hair is showing the first signs of graying at the temples. His uniform is bright blue and brings out the dark circles under his eyes. For a split second, Miranda wonders what his story is: new dad perhaps, or struggling writer burning the candle at both ends. His name tag reads Vic.

"Hey, Vic. You wouldn't happen to know where the first aid kits are by chance?" she asks.

"Aisle 7."

She freezes, and for a moment they stare at each other without another word. A second of something akin to recognition flashes in his eyes.

"What the fu . . ." she begins to say as a scream echoes from another aisle. She turns away.

"Not yet," she curses under her breath.

In moments, they will all be screaming, the piercing wails of the dying. A sound she can feel in her bones. She needs answers, though. Turning back to face Vic, he's gone. She goes around the corner, looking up and down two aisles.

"Where . . ."

She replays the interaction again and again, always landing on the same thing: she had used his name. It couldn't be that simple. Could it? She remembers Miss Rivera, the sound just before she vanished down the stairs. Maybe whatever was missing had already slipped away. Could the missing link be people forgetting who they were? Had humanity simply forgotten how to be human?

Before she can think further, a woman walks right into her path. Long, painful screams rip out of her as the flesh begins to melt from her bones. The woman's knees buckle, and she slides to the floor so smoothly it's almost like she is falling through it.

Covering her ears, Miranda runs. She isn't close enough to the front door for a clean break. Instead, she pops out the emergency fire exit. The door bursts open in silence. No alarms to go off. No one is there to be annoyed by her dramatic departure.

The door opens into a dark alley, and the sour smell of mildew and trash. Her breath catches in her throat, half due to the overwhelming odor and the other half out of fear.

There is an alley to her right, where trucks pull in to make deliveries at the loading dock. The left leads to a small parking lot filled with dumpsters. She goes to the right.

The air buzzes with static, making the hair on her arms stand on end. Her lungs burn, and her heart rate elevates. Something isn't right.

"Just get to the street," she tells herself out loud, hoping the sound of her own voice will cut through the building tension.

CRACK!

The sound makes Miranda jump and freeze mid-step, gripping the straps of her backpack tighter. She wishes she had stayed in her apartment. Leaving her familiar neighborhood was a mistake. Trying to get out of the city was an even bigger mistake.

She takes another step, and another. A light bulb explodes above her head, sending glass shards into her hair and cutting her cheek. She gives a sharp, startled scream and covers her face too late.

Continuing to walk forward more tenuously, the shadows elongate. They fill the path before her with darkness until she can no longer see her own feet. Sweat collects at her hairline and drips down her face, burning her eyes.

Sliding from the shadows, a child steps directly into her path. It's a small girl with her hair in a ponytail, wearing a pink dress covered in colorful rainbows. Her hands are clasped behind her back, and she smiles at Miranda in the mischievous way kids do.

The girl is more solid than the ghosts inside. Not a good sign. She reaches for the gun again. Sensing Miranda's intent, the girl reveals her hands. She is holding a long-handled axe. The weapon is over half her size. A playful giggle escapes her.

"I wouldn't try it, sweetheart," Miranda says, aiming the gun.

The girl's body twists and contorts before splitting in half. Blood and pus oozes onto the concrete. From the carnage, steps a large figure like a freshly birthed calf and picks up the axe.

Miranda fights the urge to lower her weapon. It's her father, right down to the scar that crossed his left eyebrow. Every detail is impeccable. That is, except for the eyes. There is something off about them, colder.

"Put the gun down," it tells her, in her father's voice.

"No," she replies.

"It will only hurt for a second. I promise. And then, we can be together again. Don't you want to be with me . . . and Mom?"

He takes a step closer.

"You're not my father. I know my father, and you're not him."

"How about now? Would this be more to your liking?" the creature says in a higher octave.

He reaches up and digs his fingers into his eye sockets. In a solid motion, he pulls down the skin, as if removing a mask. Blood and fluid pour from the sockets as laughter fills the air. With a disjointed series of pops, his spine snaps down the back like a zipper. The old flesh is discarded to the side, and Miranda looks at a perfect copy of herself.

Naked, covered in blood, and gripping the axe handle, the creature begins running towards her. Miranda fires the gun. Unphased, it swings the head of the axe so close to her face that she feels a slight breeze as she throws herself to the side.

Again, she pulls the trigger. This time, it's empty, leaving her nothing to do but throw it at the reflection of herself. It bounces off its chest, unbothered. It raises the axe again. Miranda rolls out of the way and scrambles to her feet at the sound of metal against concrete.

Grabbing the lid of a trash can, she throws it up in front of her face in time for a jarring thwack that rattles up her arms. Swinging the lid, she makes contact, and the axe goes tumbling to the ground. If she can get the weapon, she can get away. One thing she has learned about Cat:3s is that they eventually fizzle out, just like a fire. The more energy they expend, the faster they fall.

They both lunge for the weapon. Miranda is faster, but only by seconds. Both of their hands grip the handle. A quick twist and the head of the axe cracks against the side of her double's face. It falls backwards, and Miranda is on top of it. Twisting and pulling at the weapon, she's finally able to free it. She lifts the axe and, with all her strength, brings it down right between its eyes. Laughter mixes with blood and bits of brain tissue as she lifts the blade and swings again. Is it the creature's laughter or her own? She can't tell.

Again and again, she plows the metal into its skull until there's nothing left but the laughter. Dizzy with adrenaline and with the taste of blood on her lips, she stumbles down the alley. The sound of her footsteps on the pavement echoes off the buildings surrounding her. As she rounds the corner, she is flooded with the familiar once again.

The cycle is not yet complete. The roads are no longer quiet as the souls of people flood out of the doorways. Some sink to their knees, groaning, while others stand gap-mouthed like fish with no words staring up at the sky. She walks faster. Her head swims, and the earth tilts.

The world is weeping just as the man in the mural, she thinks. As she turns to look at him one last time, warm tears stream down her face; her legs buckle as she reads the words written in black spray paint beneath her own.

"Not alone."

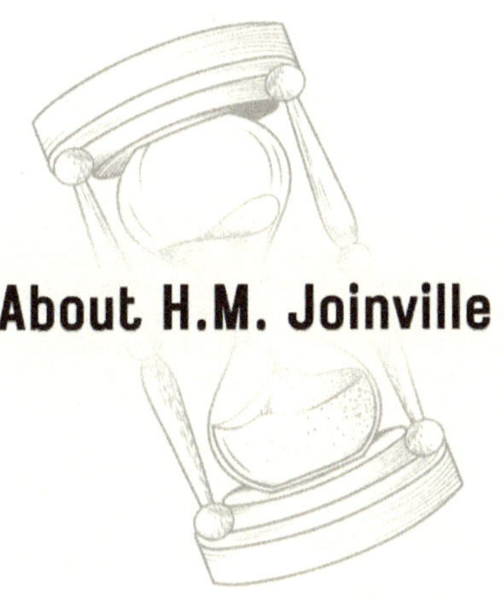

About H.M. Joinville

H.M. Joinville is a graduate of Southern Illinois University with a degree in Creative Writing. She has poetry published in Bookends Review, Best of Bookends Review 2020, and Athena Review. Carb lover at heart, she is also ordained in the Church of the Flying Spaghetti Monster. H.M. can be found on BlueSky @hmjoinville.bsky.social and on Instagram @h.m.joinville

The Unwritten Story of Their Life

by Toshiya Kamei

I KICK OFF THE BLANKET, sleep now an impossible task, and grab my phone. Opening the diary app, I let the cursor blink for a few seconds before I begin. I hope you're doing well, Ted. To me, you're what Kitty was to Anne Frank in her secret annex.

Headlights swing across the blinds, washing over the bedroom walls. The sheets lie in a crumpled heap on the half-empty bed. When I sit up cross-legged, Miss Whiskers crawls into my lap and curls into a ball. The phantom heat of Rosario's skin returns, singeing me.

Earlier today, dozens of protesters had marched past our downtown apartment building, carrying blue and pink signs and yelling "Stop Nameless hate!" Clasping the jade necklace around my neck, I had stood petrified at the window, watching my allies draped in Nameless flags, indistinguishable from transgender flags from this distance.

It doesn't help that Governor Patrick keeps cloning himself. I've lost count, but his third or fourth clone currently rules Texas. What if the cloning goes wrong and something even worse claims his seat of power?

Ted, my thoughts spiral when I'm alone.

My Rosario is a whole ocean away, visiting somewhere in Asia. Is she thinking of me now? I press my fingers to my lips, recalling the warmth of our goodbye kiss. The love aching when our lips met.

Many of us became Nameless in inconspicuous ways over the last few years. Some have speculated Big Pharma is behind it, somehow targeting those of us who received hormone therapy, but nothing conclusive has ever surfaced.

The latest flu pandemic broke the dyke holding back hatred for the Nameless. Many in our community have turned to essential work in hospitals and grocery stores, working long hours under poor conditions for little pay. Nameless toiling in farms and meat-packing plants get blamed for transmitting zoonotic influenza to humans. With each wave of infection, we become easy scapegoats. Violent attacks against us have spiked and lives have been lost.

Experts estimate that 1.6 million Americans are Nameless. Many stay in the closet to avoid discrimination.

The summer between eleventh and twelfth grade, I met my first serious girlfriend, Rocío, at the fast food restaurant where we both worked. Everyone called her Maria, however. She was Undocumented, so like Nameless today, she lived under a false name. I didn't learn her true name until we started hanging around her home in the evenings after work.

"Bienvenida — estás en tu casa." As soon as Rocío stepped inside, she reverted to Spanish, leaving her English for the outside world — like how my Japanese ancestors removed their shoes when they entered their homes. My name melted like sweet fruit on her tongue. If I weren't Nameless, I'd be able to remember the taste of her kiss.

"¿Estás cansada?" she asked.

I shook my head. In reality, I was exhausted, but the melodious sonority of her Spanish enchanted me. And to my delight, the feminine adjective — cansada — affirmed my gender.

Spanish, a gendered language, allowed me to reclaim my femininity. I was no longer a crossdresser with an effeminate manner. My feminine adjectives could attest to that.

We sat on the couch. I rested my head on her shoulder, the sweet floral scent of her hair filling my nose, while we watched a telenovela in her living room. Sra. García, Rocío's mother, joined us when she came home.

I don't remember which series was on that night, but it starred Aracely Arámbula as a successful businesswoman seeking revenge against the men who murdered her father when she was a young girl.

Soon, binge-watching telenovelas together became part of our dating routine. Rocío and I would devour everything Aracely Arámbula was in, teasing each other about our infatuation with the Mexican actress.

"Ya me voy a costar." Sra. García yawned, covering her mouth, and rose to her feet.

"Descansa, mamita." My girlfriend craned her neck and gave her mother a goodnight kiss.

"Pórtense bien, niñas." Sra. García wore a mischievous grin, wagging her finger. She added that she had Rocío when Sra. García was Rocío's age; as far as she was concerned, though, she was too young to be an abuela.

"Sí, mami, no te preocupes." Rocío waved away her mother's worry.

"Maria, why does your mom call you Rocío?" I asked after Sra. García disappeared into her bedroom. I fidgeted in Rocío's embrace when a tampon commercial came on TV. Those days, any mention of feminine hygiene products ate away at my self-confidence, making me feel different from other girls.

She remained silent, but her faraway gaze told me she was weighing her options.

"Is that your middle name?"

"Es que me llamo Rocío, me llamo así por mi abuela." She

removed the heart-shaped pendant from her neck and showed me a sepia studio photo of her abuela.

"May I call you Rocío?" I said, reaching out to cup her left cheek.

"Claro, mi amor." She beamed, and her pearly teeth shimmered.

When she kissed me, it felt like she'd handed me a key to her heart.

Even today, her name makes me think of a dewdrop sparkling in the morning sun.

I, for one, can't cope with the stress of hiding my identity, so I choose to be out. Whenever I go outside, I'm required to wear an armband indicating my status as Nameless. They say the armbands help the authorities identify us in case we get lost, but I don't buy that. They want to track us. They don't want us to explore, like I used to as a child.

Left in Grandma's care all day, I grew up speaking Japanese. More specifically, onna kotoba, or women's language. Under her sweet, grandmotherly gaze, I blossomed into girlhood on my terms, and Japanese played no small part in articulating my gender.

Our favorite hangout was the Fort Worth Japanese Garden, and we would spend hours exploring the 7.5 acres strewn with sakura, kaede, bamboo, and magnolias. We would drop quarters in the fish-food dispenser and grab fistfuls of pellets. We always chuckled as koi swam up to the surface to nibble food from our fingers.

Grandma — would also take me to a small neighborhood park where I would have play dates with Misa, a young Meg Tilly look-alike.

"Your Japanese is girly," Misa said. The chains squeaked and creaked as my grandmother and Misa's mother pushed the swings.

"That's because I'm a girl," I said, sticking my chest out. "Isn't that so, Grandma?" I looked back toward her.

"That's right, my darling girl," my grandmother said. Her eyes disappeared into a warm smile.

"See?" I said proudly. We swung up and down, drawing arcs.

"Okay." Misa shrugged, still unconvinced. Even so, she never commented on my Japanese after that.

Sadly, I lost much of my Japanese after Grandma passed away the day I turned five. That was when I decided to name myself after her, like Sra. García named her daughter after her mother, partly to honor my grandmother's life and partly to embrace my authentic self.

Clad in black mourning clothes, my parents took turns hugging me, celebrating that I'd claimed my identity. It was nothing out of the ordinary. Prior to Westernization in the latter half of the twentieth century, Japanese viewed biological sex as a spectrum. Besides, many overseas Japanese have middle names we inherited from our ancestors like yaeba, sticking out like a mouthful of chalk.

I loved Grandma. When I was three, she bought me a little girl's kimono for the Shichi-Go-San Festival. Dressed in the pink silk kimono patterned with flowers, I threw my arms around her neck and showered her with kisses. It's one of the most meaningful gifts I've received.

A miserable year of Saturday Japanese school in Dallas, when I was seven years old, was no help; I was bullied so badly I had to drop out.

Now, I have no one to practice with. No one besides AI.

"I love you, Grandma," I say to the microphone.

"Obachan, daisuki." The app translates my input and speaks in an AI-generated voice that sounds like mine.

I'm a lost cause, but Rosario's Spanish is quite salvageable. She says she's embarrassed about not being fluent, but most words are on the tip of her tongue. I want her to whisper sweet nothings to me in Spanish while we cuddle and kiss. Is that too much to ask, Ted? In my book, Spanish is the most romantic language in the world. La lengua del amor. Do you agree?

I'll talk her into enrolling in Zoom classes together at Spanish Sin Pena when she gets back. I love Wendy Ramírez's enthusiasm. Dressed in a white huipil, she assures prospective students that we can have fun learning Spanish while healing from the pains of assimilation. Her school also organizes cultural immersion tours of Chiapas, hitting all the hot spots like the temple-pyramids at Palenque.

Steeped in Mayan culture, the southernmost state of Mexico provides sanctuary to the Nameless. Since their initial uprising in 2014, the Zapatistas, a group of mostly indigenous activists, have come to control a third of its territory. Rosario Castellanos, my favorite poet, grew up in Comitán, near the border of Guatemala. Her indigenista novels address the plight of Chiapaneco indigenous people, and her poetry is the diary of her life. The ancient Maya worshipped several divine felines, most importantly the Jaguar God of Terrestrial Fire. Hopefully, as cat parents, Rosario and I will be welcome in Chiapas.

I hug Miss Whiskers close to me like a pillow, remembering how blessed I have been — Anne wasn't allowed to take her cat with her into hiding.

Kafka, another favorite diarist of mine, was also Jewish. We all read *The Metamorphosis* in high school. My English teacher, Mrs. Palomo, said Kafka's work anticipated the Holocaust. Born in the Jewish ghetto in Prague, he was excluded from the German minority in the city. Although Kafka died in 1924, years before the "Final Solution," his immediate relatives were annihilated by the Nazis during World War II. *The Metamorphosis* is relatable to me on a personal level. In it, Gregor Samsa is belittled, harmed, and ultimately murdered for his transformation. No one has tried to physically harm me for being Nameless, mind you, but I can imagine how Kafka might have felt.

I've been a stay-at-home cat mom since I lost my call center job to automation. Being freed from that tedious gig came as a relief. Rosario works as an IT security consultant and travels around the world, leaving me alone with Miss Whiskers for long stretches of time. She never reveals her precise destinations, let alone the nature of her duties. It's for our safety, she says. She sounds like a secret agent.

Here's a bit of good news, though: we're jump-starting our family thanks to student loan debt relief, monthly UBI payments, and universal healthcare. I rarely go out these days, and being a housewife suits me fine. Rosario is eighteen weeks pregnant, and Uncle Sam will pay me to look after our child until they turn eighteen.

I've already picked a name for the baby. It's a unisex name. I want to save ourselves the potential heartache and paperwork. Call me superstitious, but I won't reveal the name to anyone, not even to my diary. Or to you, Ted.

The other day, I painted the nursery purple while listening to Prince's wailing guitar. My partner and I both love the Purple One. We hired a Prince tribute band for our engagement party and ordered a purple velvet cake for the gender reveal party. The baker told us they used powdered purple yam for its coloring.

Rosario is a girl's name meaning "rosary" in Spanish, but it's also given to boys in Italy in honor of Saint Dominic, a Castilian priest credited with inventing the rosary for Catholic worship. So, Rosario is a unisex name — no disrespect to my mother-in-law who named her child after herself.

My Rosario's pronouns are she/they, but she can easily pass as a cishet woman. I have no illusion about passing as non-Nameless, however. What if someone asks my name? I'd have to give them a false one if I didn't want them to know I'm Nameless.

Rosario is the brave one. I call her my ninja because she accesses places off-limits to the Nameless. Given the nature of her work, she can't share much, but she's often sent on missions to exotic locales. She visited Taipei earlier this year and brought me back the jade necklace along with local sweets. A whole bag of peanut nougat was gone in a matter of minutes, but the necklace still hangs around my neck. It never comes off if I can help it. Speaking of Taiwan, I imagine you visited your grandparents there while growing up. Maybe for a book tour? I've always wondered what your Chinese name means.

It breaks my heart to report that my parents aren't happy about our pregnancy.

My mom's first reaction: "My darling. Why would you want to bring a child into this hellscape? Adopting a kitten wasn't enough for you two?"

Miss Whiskers meows in my lap. She meows when she thinks we're talking about her.

Every Zoom call from my mom turns into a nag session. She accuses me of defecting to the dark side. As far as she's concerned, I'm a modern-day June Cleaver.

"You don't want to be a traitor to feminism, do you? You should be mindful of the sacrifices previous generations made."

I cope with her sermon by retreating into my sexual fantasy, imagining Rosario whispering "déjame hacerte el amor," her breath tickling my ear.

My dad complains he didn't send me to college for this. "My baby girl. I thought you went to grad school for an MFA, not an MRS." He even sent me a vasectomy brochure.

I'm still hurt. I cry when I'm alone. Even so, Rosario and I are going forward with our pregnancy.

On the night of our engagement, after our guests had gone home, we were left alone in our apartment. Like Louise and her husband from "Story of Your Life," Rosario and I slow-danced like a teenage couple in the moonlight seeping through the window. I drew back and gazed at her in the dim glow before kissing her on the lips. Maybe it was the wine we drank to celebrate our engagement. Or maybe it was pixie dust in the spring air. Something prompted Rosario to ask: *Do you want to make a baby?*

"Tómame, Rosario," I begged in a raspy voice. "Hazme tuya, por favor." A wave of desire coursed through me as she caressed my hair, kissed my neck, and bit my earlobe.

That night, our baby was conceived. Rosario and I will tell

them the PG-13 version of this story when they're ready to start a family of their own. Unlike Louise, though, neither of us knows how our story ends.

As I write, Ted, a rerun of a telenovela is playing on TV. The theme song reaches a crescendo, and Aracely Arámbula's voice soars as she repeats the refrain, declaring herself to be the owner of her lover's heart. I hum along as best as I can, imagining myself resting my head against Rosario's shoulder, her dulcet fragrance tickling my nostrils.

I wonder if you ever jolt awake after midnight, bolt out of bed, and scramble to find your cat for comfort. I've found my kitten, but I can't get back to sleep. Alone on my side of bed, I trace the dent in the mattress where my fiancé usually sleeps.

My fiancé. It sounds like something out of the pages of the lesbian pulp I devoured as a teenager. Unless I'm with my Spanish-speaking in-laws, I prefer the gender-neutral term. "Fiancée" looks even more old-fashioned.

Nearly a decade ago, I befriended Rosario at Index Writers' Group.

Do you like Rosario Castellanos? I slid into her DMs, hoping for an affirmative answer.

Hmm . . . who's that?

The answer was disappointing, but it didn't dissuade me.

She wrote a poem called "Apelación al solitario."

Never heard of it.

The speaker of the poem says you have to find a companion now and then; you can't be born alone, nor can you die alone. So, I'm wondering if you're single.

Are you hitting on me?

Guilty as charged.

Despite this initial misstep, she and I eventually bonded over our mutual love for Ranma. While chatting on WhatsApp, I said Ranma is a trans girl like me, and she sent me a heart emoji. We then collaborated on a fanfic in which Ranma and Akane lived in marital bliss with a baby on the way. We posted it online under our joint pseudonym: Akane Saotome. I think it's still up on AO3.

Even separated by several states, Rosario and I found pleasure in teasing each other by co-writing gay smut. We would use Google Docs and work on a shared document from our respective bedrooms.

A few weeks later, we met at Chicon 8 where we geeked out in costumes and roomed together to save expenses.

My heart jackhammered in my chest as the cab dropped me off at the Hyatt. *Arrived!* I typed, but I didn't send it. A part of me wanted to surprise her. Wanted to sneak up behind her and wrap my arms around her waist.

I checked in and went straight to room 213. When I knocked at the door, Rosario appeared in her Akane cosplay. I was nearly a foot taller.

"—!" Rosario beamed. "I'm so happy you're here!"

We squeaked and hugged. She fussed over me as I put on my Ranma costume: a red sleeveless shirt with a Mandarin collar, a red ponytail wig, and black pants. She sat me on the bed and leaned forward, her face almost touching mine. A tingle rushed through me when our knees grazed. We breathed the same air, nearly kissing. I felt like a teenager all over again, like when I was with Rocío. With a fluttering heart, I took in her sweet scent as she lined my eyes in purple liner.

The convention, brimming with fellow nerds, immediately felt welcoming. After an exhausting day hopping from one panel to another, we slipped into separate beds, but I found her curled next to me in the morning.

That same weekend, we climbed Sears Tower together. I enjoyed exploring a new city as much as anyone else back then. Even so, we didn't climb the stairs. All 2,109 steps? Rosario could have, but I wouldn't have survived. We took the high-speed elevator instead.

Somewhere downtown, afraid of getting lost, I approached

someone who looked like a local. By local, I mean a normie as opposed to a geek like me.

"Excuse me. Are you from around here?" I said. "Can you tell us how to get to Willis Tower?"

"You mean Sears Tower," the young man said. Adjusting his well-worn Cubs cap, he gave us directions.

"Can you help me out a bit?" he asked when I thanked him. "I need to buy cigarettes."

Rosario nudged me to move on, but I thought it was bad karma not to repay his kindness.

"Is it enough?" I pulled a crisp sawbuck from my purse and slipped it into his hand.

"Much appreciated." He pocketed the money and melted into the crowd.

"You could've thanked him and walked away," Rosario said.

"I don't mind being a pushover," I said. "Besides, my neck was hurting from gazing up."

"You ditzy girl!" Rosario chuckled. "The entrance is on the ground!"

I decided to let her lead the way. I'm horrible at directions. Once, while driving on the freeway in the Bay Area, I almost entered a ramp from the wrong direction. Good thing I wasn't behind the wheel this time. Chicago is full of one-way streets.

Rosario and I shuffled into the tower's elevator along with other tourists. My stomach tightened as we sped up. My ears popped as I swallowed. A glance at Rosario confirmed that her ears had done the same. Our bodies clumped together against the back wall, and her curves pressed against my body. When I met her coal-dark eyes, my cheeks burned. We giggled and gave each other pecks on the lips during the rest of our ascent.

When we reached the 103rd floor, the doors slid open and spat us out. We kissed again, for longer, on the observation deck. My knees almost buckled.

Mustering our courage, we stepped onto the glass box

suspended 1,353 feet in the air. Rosario's fingers felt cold against my sweaty palm. I clung to her arm to steady myself.

Blue-green Lake Michigan glistened on the horizon, and I kept my eyes half-closed until she led me back down to Earth. My pulse quickens every time I recall that Saturday.

We maintained a long-distance relationship for a couple of years, and she eventually came to live with me here in Fort Worth around the time I became Nameless. She's been by my side ever since.

Don't get me wrong, I love her, but there's something bothering me. She doesn't speak Spanish to me.

Rosario is calling me now, Ted. She only addresses me by pet names; she doesn't want to remind me of the fact that I've lost my name. Most of the time, she makes me feel safe and protected, but there are times I feel she's coddling me.

"Hey, girlie, what are you doing?" Rosario asks, smiling at the phone camera. Her smile freezes for a moment, but I wave it off as a technical glitch. Her jet-black hair is tied into a tight ponytail, and she looks sharp in her business blazer. Growing up, I had a thing for curvy girls like her, and I always say she could make a killing as a body-positive influencer if she ever got fired. It's daytime where she is, and she's seated somewhere outdoors with feeble trees behind her. Children cheer outside the frame.

"I'm talking to Ted," I tell her.

"You're busy then?" She frowns, looking a bit worried.

"Not really. I miss you, mi mamita chula."

Every chance I get, I make a point of calling her by a Spanish pet name, letting her know I crave feminine adjectives.

"Te amo," I say, hoping she'll respond in Spanish. "¿Verdad que soy tu nena?"

"Of course, baby. I love you, too."

I lift Miss Whiskers from my lap and make her wave.

"Can't you come home now?"

"I wish I could, love." She laughs, and the worried look disappears from her face. "I just got out of a yawn-inducing meeting.

An American tech startup is setting up a new office here in Tokyo, and they want me to train the local team."

Negative thoughts slip into my mind with a ninja's stealth. The vastness of the Pacific Ocean divides us, like tanabata lovers separated by the Milky Way. A sudden melancholy grabs my chest.

"Rosario, mi amor." Tears ring in my voice.

"What's the matter, baby?" She frowns, and the children playing in the background let out bright peals of laughter. Will our child laugh like that? Will they know joy? My mother's warning hovers like a dark cloud over me.

"I'm nervous about naming our child," I say.

I don't know what she expected me to say, but her frown melts into a smile.

"Don't worry, sweetie. You'll do fine."

"But what if they lose their name too?" Knowing that being Nameless isn't hereditary fails to make me feel any better.

"That's not going to happen," Rosario says, biting her lower lip. "I can promise you that."

I breathe out slowly. Miss Whiskers is a warm, solid weight. A counterbalance to my spiraling thoughts. I know no one can promise safety. Everyone thought names were intrinsic. That identities could never be taken away. We were wrong. But I know Rosario is only trying to help.

"Thank you, Rosario. It's reassuring to hear that."

Another smile, but as soon as our eyes meet, she looks away. Off to the side. A bird glides in the sky, and puffy clouds drift across the blue.

"Is anything good on TV?" Rosario asks.

"Aracely Arámbula is starring in a new telenovela. It's a sequel of some sort. A remake, rather. I want us to watch it together."

"You've got the wrong Rosario, baby," she says. "You should call my mom. That's right up her alley."

"Rosario, no seas mala," I say with feigned resentment.

"You win." Throwing up her hands, she rolls her eyes, but her smile seems off. I sit up.

"What's wrong?"

She blinks once, and a fleeting edge of surprise flashes in her eyes before her expression turns serious.

"You're too good at reading me. I didn't know if I was going to bring it up now — I should probably wait to tell you in person — but someone contacted me. She goes by Momoko."

"The notorious hacker?" I frown. "Why?"

"What I mean is . . . she contacted Akane Saotome."

Akane Saotome. Our nom de plume.

Once, we got a kick out of writing a tribute to your story "Understand." In our homage, a Fort Worth-based empath desperately seeks her missing lover. That is, until the femme fatale reappears — shedding her disguise and assuming her true identity — and initiates the empath's downfall.

My stomach curdles at the thought of Rosario facing her own downfall, and not only because she's pregnant. I can't lose mi vida. I can't live in a world where she no longer exists.

"She tells me two heads are better than one," Rosario finally says. "She wants me to team up with her."

"Why?" I ask, confused. "What does she want?"

"Her partner was prescribed birth control pills for acne."

"Let me guess," I say, cold sweat running down my spine. "She's Mumei — Nameless."

"Yeah." Rosario pauses, pensive. "This almost feels like one of our plots, doesn't it?" Clouds obscure the sun, and her skin becomes sickly pale in the sudden gloom.

"Art imitates life," I say. "Or is it the other way around?"

If there's one thing I learned from my old day job, it's that almost anything can be sugarcoated. For instance, despite a lack of actual intelligence, AI has been deemed as such. Names matter, and the right one makes any pill easy to swallow.

"What did you agree to, Rosario?"

"Momoko says there's only one company that manufactures birth control pills in Japan. It's Hikari Pharma."

I wish I knew what was coming, Ted. I wish I could do anything but stare at the screen as my heart pounds.

"Her hypothesis is that the algorithm controlling the drug manufacturing process has somehow become corrupted. Momoko believes it's possible to hack into Hikati Pharma's system, isolate the corruption, and fix it."

The wind plasters dark strands of hair across Rosario's forehead. My lips go numb as I try to speak.

"You can't do this, Rosario. If they catch you. Or if someone finds out—"

"I have to try! Baby, I want you whole again. I want you to be freed from this."

I don't so much as flinch, but her tone softens.

"You are whole. I didn't mean it like that. I just mean . . . I want to get back what you lost."

I exhale a shaky breath and swallow.

"Even if you found concrete evidence," I say, "I'm sure nobody would believe you. And a lawsuit against a deep-pocketed drug company would be truly quixotic. A sympathetic judge might order an independent audit of the drug company's servers, but you'd need proof. Not conjecture."

"Right."

"What are you going to do, Rosario?" Tears well up, but I don't want her to see me crying.

"You already know the answer to that."

"Be careful, Rosario. We have to think of our baby."

"I know," she says. "I know."

I remain silent because there's nothing else left to say. It's her love for me that's making her take this risk.

"I'm going to talk to Momoko and find out more." She glances at her wristwatch.

"Okay, take care, mi nena," I say with fake cheer as I blow her a kiss out of habit. "We still have to enroll in Spanish Sin Pena," I manage to say before Rosario hangs up.

To distract myself, I grab the dog-eared copy of *Stories of Your*

Life and Others from the night table. I trace the dedication Rosario inked on the book plate: *To my Ranma.*

I'm okay with not being able to write anything as perfect. You know, I tried to imitate you, Ted, when I was a teenager. To me, writing has always been personal. My writing is an extension of myself, and no algorithm will replace that. So, unlike my day job, writing can't be eliminated by automation as long as I'm alive.

Many loved your *New Yorker* articles on technology for what they were: love letters to humanity. Celebrations of human creativity. I'm no exception.

Despite the nefarious ways in which humans use bots — we've all seen the viral videos of the police unleashing robo-dogs on Nameless protesters — you taught us never to be afraid. You reminded us that bots are inanimate objects, no matter what AI adherents say. They're not tsukumogami — tools that have acquired spirits in Japanese folklore.

I was inspired when you said everyone writes clunkers. Revision was my jam, so I remained firmly in the AI skeptic camp. After getting feedback from my betas, I would spend hours making multiple rounds of revisions, chiseling away superfluous asides like this.

Maybe it's this optimism that keeps me writing to you. If you can be optimistic about our collective future, I can be optimistic about getting my name back. Is this a stretch?

Life, though, was far from perfect even before I became Nameless. When I began submitting my short stories, many editors excluded me from women-only projects. They said I wasn't a real woman.

Of course, I wasn't the only one who was misgendered. A nonbinary poet was forced to withdraw their accepted pieces when the editor objected to the singular use of "they" in their short bio, saying the English major in her couldn't tolerate such a grammatical transgression. When I tweeted *Humans aren't binary* in the poet's support, I got kicked off the bird site.

None of this was good, but I still wish I could go back to how things were. At least I had a name. As Nameless are still figuring out ways to convey our lost identities to the world, I can see why many of us are fascinated by how your fiction explores new ways to communicate.

"Story of Your Life" further confirms this simple fact: all knowledge isn't phonetically based. Linguist Louise Banks can't decipher the alien language from an audio recording alone; she has to visit the landing site to interact with native speakers. In fact, Flapper and Raspberry communicate through semagrams which convey ideas independently from speech.

God granted humans the ability to name, per Judeo-Christian tradition, but humans have abused that privilege over and over. Naming is a form of ownership. Colonizers pillaged the continent and renamed it "America." The enslaved were given the names of whoever owned them. Their identities, gone. Even Sears Tower was renamed when the building changed hands.

Humans have transmuted pride into arrogance. Throughout history, the Victor Frankensteins of the world have tried to play God. With chatbots, AI developers will fail again. As for the alchemist extraordinaire, he didn't even bother to name his monster.

You have an uncanny knack for naming your work. I, on the other hand, am hopelessly inept at it. I can't go with "Untitled" every time I write in my diary. An early draft began as "Dear Ted," and I went from "Nameless Lives Matter" to "My Gender Is a Blurry JPEG" before settling on this current one.

But as I write you, Ted, I keep returning to how the police use canine robots to hunt down their suspects. They believe the purpose of bots is to remind us of our subjugation. Proof that we're cogs in the machine. I can't go along with that, of course. Human creativity is magic, as is faith. And technology is part of this equation too — as we reach for what's impossible, we figure out ways to conceptualize the possible.

Like finding a cure for the Nameless.

My phone shakes, alerting me to Rosario's call. It's just her checking in, as she often does.

The next day, Rosario calls again. But as soon as I answer, I know something is different. Rosario's expression is exuberant, joyful. She beams next to a serious-looking Asian woman around my age. My heart starts to race.

"What is it, Rosario? What's going on?"

"Baby, guess what? Momoko and I have done it!"

The stranger — Momoko — wears thin-rimmed glasses, and her hair is cut in a short bob. Her smile reads smug. Corky. For some reason, that makes me frown.

"What have you done?"

"We located the bug in Hikari Pharma's servers," Momoko says. "The bug evaded discovery for years by mutating, but I knew it couldn't hide forever."

"A bug? But what does that mean, Rosario?" Tears prick my eyes, but I blink them back. "What about my name?"

"This proves that not every job can be automated," Momoko continues, as if she didn't hear me. "And it won't be, considering the cost of bot implementation."

"I won't bore you with the details," Rosario says, "but we cracked their firewalls and reverse-engineered an antidote. Hopefully, Hikari Pharma will voluntarily recall the defective drugs from the market. Otherwise, Momoko will have to twist their arms."

Momoko smiles like she wishes the Hikari Pharma CEOs would allow her to do just that.

"I can't wait to see you," Rosario says. "And I can't wait to do the same with Big Pharma when I get home."

"I can't wait to see you either," I say. But the more I look at Rosario, the more her earlier excitement seems to dim. She cuts her gaze away from me. The world suddenly feels slippery underfoot, uncertain, and I don't know why. My stomach churns.

Somehow, I manage to speak without my voice shaking. "What's wrong, Rosario? What is it? Tell me what's wrong."

When Rosario looks at me again, she doesn't bother to hide her tears.

"Baby, we can't help those already afflicted. We can only prevent future cases. That means—"

I know what it means. My nails dig into my palm as Rosario and Momoko cross the street, pedestrians hemming them in. As we say goodbye. As the screen goes dark.

I'll remain Nameless for the foreseeable future.

Even so, our baby will be safe. I repeat their name a few times through tears, and I squeeze Miss Whiskers tight. She meows and licks my wet cheeks. Fingers still trembling, I send Rosario a heart emoji.

We live in a topsy-turvy world where nothing makes sense. But you've taught us that already, Ted.

When morning comes, I'll step outside and join my Nameless allies on the march.

Eventually, we Nameless will find a non-phonetic way to convey our names to others. Maybe through semagrams like Flapper and Raspberry.

Rosario will come home soon, and I'll tell her our child's name, whispering it in her ear as we tumble toward the couch. She'll love the name as much as I do. We'll book the Fort Worth Japanese Garden for our wedding, praying for a sunny day. We'll go to Chiapas for our honeymoon, and we'll interact with native Spanish speakers. Back in our hotel room, she'll whisper "déjame hacerte el amor" as we make love. I'll learn a few lullabies in Japanese, the ones Grandma used to sing to me, before the baby is born. And everything will be perfect. Ted. So perfect.

Warmly,

Nameless

About Toshiya Kamei

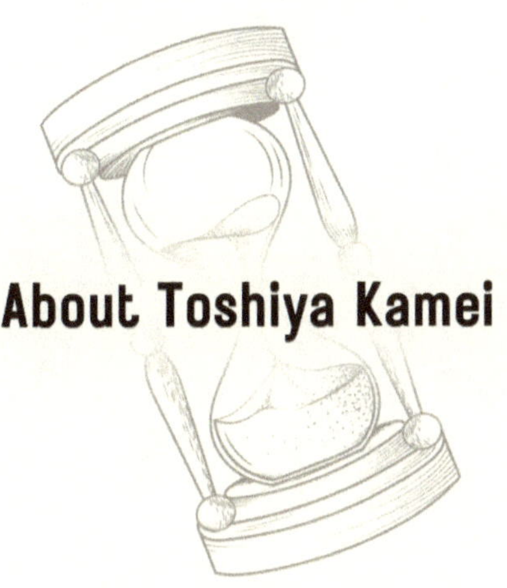

Toshiya Kamei (she/her) is a queer Asian writer who takes inspiration from fairy tales, folklore, and mythology.

Live a Little

by Rayleigh Call

"COME IN, Osage. This is Whiskey. Five. Whiskey. Bravo. Juliet. Over."

My heart knocks against my ribs, impatient for a response.

Static crackles, then Ida's rusty drawl resonates through the speaker. "Copy, Warren Bunker J. This is Whiskey. Five. Oscar. Sierra. Alpha. Good to hear yer voice, baby! Over."

I push out a breath and slide the microphone closer. "How're things, Auntie? Over."

"Oh, same old. And how's yer dad — ope!" Her voice catches as she realizes her mistake. "You gotta forgive this old lady. Orders're way up since we signed on with a new supplier. Great for business, but it takes all my energy jus' stayin' upright on two feet. Over."

I smile and nod, though she obviously can't see me. "I get it, Auntie. I forget Pops is gone, too. Over." Only been six weeks. Not sure I'll ever get used to it.

"Hm. How 'bout the hydroponics? Got the pump parts I sent ya installed? Over."

"Not just yet, but I'm fixin' to start planting before summer closes. Over."

"I see. Well, give a holler if ya need anythin'. Gopher life ain't for everybody. Over."

Gopher, huh? Never heard Ida say a rude word or speak unkindly of bunker dwellers before, though I find the term more ignorant than offensive. I can't understand why surface folks think living underground is so crazy. At least down here the air and water are clean, and there are no tornadoes or bandits. I'll take monotony over that kind of trouble any day.

When I don't respond, Ida pivots back to business. "Got yer supply list ready? Over."

Putting her comment out of my mind, I position the pad in front of me and read slowly down the line. Ida chimes in with out-of-stock notices and substitution suggestions. No peaches, as usual. Waxed apples instead of pears. Add lentils to long beans to bulk the order and replace brown rice with oats. I'm heartbroken there's no meat or dairy — not that there ever is — but she offers two cases of fresh eggs at cost to supplement the powdered stuff.

"As for payment . . ." She hesitates, no doubt grasping for a sympathetic way to remind me Pops's credit is depleted. Used the last on the parts and those good-for-nothing antibiotics.

"I can trade this time," I say proudly. "Oyster and shiitake mushrooms. Three pounds each. And," I pause like I'm cueing a drum roll for the big reveal, "truffles. Two ounces black and one white. Over." Sitting back in Pops's worn leather chair, I cross my fingers and wait for Ida to scan her price reference lists. Prolonged drought has made fungi a rare commodity topside. Hopefully, the trade-in value reflects the effort it took to grow them.

After a minute or two, she clicks her tongue. "That'll do it, baby. I'll move your daddy's account under your name and note the exchange on the invoice. Now, lemme check the—"

The line erupts with static. Not static. The choking, sputtering *kak, kak* of Ida's chronic cough. The sound cuts out briefly, then picks up with a forceful "*Ahem*" as she tries to laugh it off. "Shucks, musta caught a frog in my gullet! Hah!"

I wince and shift nervously in my seat. Surface folks must get sick all the time. It's the only explanation for how easy they make light of something so scary. The bug that got Pops was certainly no joke. Another reason I'm lucky to live underground.

She clears her throat. "If you can hold out a week, I'll put you down for the nineteenth. Jus' know, with the uptick in orders, I handed most of my routes over to the crew. Kid who took yers is a good one. Worked the fields a long time, so he's real strong. I'm faxin' over his license. Be sure ya pass it along to the bots at the gate, so they don't give him trouble on drop day. Over."

My jaw clenches. Is she pulling this because Pops isn't here to argue? I swallow hard and lean into the microphone. "No disrespect, Auntie. But our deal is *you* drive. If you're fixin' to send somebody else, I need time to vet their credentials and—"

"*Credentials?*" Her sharp voice cuts clean through mine. "Gophers got some nerve! Hardly any profit fillin' orders small as yers, ya know? Most caravaners don't bother, and we're the only ones still truckin' out to the Warren, given the rough route. I don't mind doin' favors now and then, but ya at least oughta act grateful for all I do so ya can stay safe in yer little holes." She coughs and adds hastily, "It ain't personal. Yer daddy'd understand. Over."

Blood thrums behind my ears. It sure feels personal. Ida and Pops didn't always agree, but she never spat acid or slung slurs when he was around. Does she talk like this to others in the Warren? Pops wasn't on the best terms with the Bunker Owners' Association, but maybe if I reached out, polled their experiences, I'd know if there's any point pushing back.

Who am I kidding? Even if I had somebody in mind to contact, there's no time for it. Until I finish repairs on the hydroponics system, I can't guarantee I'll have enough food to last through winter. And Ida's probably not exaggerating about the scarcity of delivery options in an area as remote as the Warren. It's the whole reason they built the bunkers out here. Safety in solitude.

I bite my lip and tap my fingers against the scarred oak desk.

Perhaps sensing my unease through the silence, Ida sighs and softens her tone. "Don't trouble yourself now, baby. Ya got my word. Redd'll do a good job. And if he don't, I'll whup him myself. Over."

BZZZZZZT!

The book in my hand tumbles to the floor as I spring from my bed with a start.

The robotic voice sounds through the speaker in the ceiling: "Attention. Scheduled visitor inbound. Prepare for imminent arrival."

Drop time. *Finally.*

I lace up my boots and march through the living quarters, stopping briefly to retrieve the box of mushrooms from the pantry before heading down the long hallway to the elevator portal. Popping open the gear locker, I grab Pops's black tac jacket, utility gloves, and gas mask. I yank the straps on the mask tight as they'll go and zip the oversize jacket up to my chin. It doesn't fit right, but it still smells like him. Tea tree oil and musk.

Stepping onto the elevator, I close the metal gate behind me and engage the motor. A low rumble echoes up the exposed rock shaft as the platform rises. Four floors. Three. Out of range of the bunker's climate regulator, the temperature increases sharply near the surface. Sweat beads at my forehead and soaks my clothes under the lead-lined jacket. I tug the collar and fan my face with a gloved paw, struggling to breathe normally so the inside of the mask doesn't fog up.

The arrival of the lift at the garage level triggers the lights and ventilation system. Even through the mask's filter, the space smells dusty. Deserted. Pops serviced the bots at the security gates, so he used to pass through at least once a week. First and last time I came up was when they took his body for incineration. There's no residue, no markings, no shadows to indicate its placement. But when my eyes flick to the bare concrete floor, they settle reflexively on the spot where I laid the slender, black bag to rest. I shiver despite the heat.

Concentrate! What step am I on? One was gear, two was the elevator . . . I turn to the screen showing the live feeds from the cameras mounted outside, and when the target bounces into view, I release the garage door. The motor purrs and the metal clangs as it rolls up to the ceiling, revealing the rear of the box truck silhouetted against a neon tangerine sky.

Sunset. When was the last time I saw one in person? When I was little? My memories before the bunker are sparse, but vivid. Pink clouds orbiting a park in the city. Bare feet in wet grass. Ma and Pops holding my hands.

Red brake lights flash, and the truck draws backward, skillfully stopping an inch from the loading deck. Four steps down. Now the part I'm dreading most. I can count on two hands the number of people I've had physical contact with since we moved into the bunker. Pops, of course. A few members of the Bunker Owners' Association and their families.

And now, this guy. Redd Miles.

He cuts the engine and drops from the cab, kicking the door closed as he fidgets with a red kerchief tied over the lower half of his face. He's bigger than I expected. The license Ida faxed over listed age, height, and weight all similar to mine, but this man is several inches taller and a fair bit bulkier. Odd he's not wearing any protective gear. Pops never left the bunker without his whole body covered, so I figured it was typical for surface folks, too. Besides the flimsy face covering and steel-toed work boots, the rest of his outfit is plain clothes: loose denim and a thin, black long-sleeve. I tug my collar again, seething at his relative comfort.

"H-hey!" My voice cracks and I cringe. At least my flushed

cheeks aren't visible behind my mask. I clear my throat. "I'm Rabbit White. The, uh, receiver. Good to meet you."

He climbs onto the platform a few feet away and looks me up and down. "What's with the getup?" He asks, tapping a pointed finger against my visor.

I flinch. "P-protection. Germs, toxins, radiation . . ." My heart thumps with uncertainty. "You *are* Redd Miles, yeah? From Osage Co-op?"

"Yep. That's me." He pulls the kerchief down to his neck and cracks a crooked smile. The gapped teeth, dark eyes, and straight nose are recognizable from the thumbnail on the license, though that was so gray and fuzzy I half expected him to be a dust bunny in coveralls. Dirt flecks his suntanned skin like freckles, and his black hair is tied up in a large knot at his crown. Not a style I'd imitate, but it's fine on him. Handsome, even.

Shoot, what am I thinking?

"Rabbit ain't a common name," he says, sliding his hands into his pockets and shifting his weight to one side. "Your folks call you that 'cause you live in the Warren?"

"No, I was born in the city."

"OKC? Well, all right, fancy pants. But you gotta admit it's a helluva coincidence."

I roll my eyes. Like I haven't heard that before. "Redd's just as unusual."

"It's a nickname. Don't sound so bad outta your mouth, but Rabbit's much cuter." He gives a shallow bow, slaps his thighs through the fabric of his jeans, and takes a step back. "I'd truly like to stay and talk awhile, but I'm fixin' to get back before they cut off supper service. Best get a move on." Without waiting for a response, he turns on his heel and disappears inside the truck.

I inhale deeply and stack my gloved hands on top of my head, pumping my elbows to encourage air flow to my armpits. No use. I'm hotter than a roast pig and twice as moist. The garage has cooled down some now that the sun's set, but the adrenaline coursing through my veins is making sweat pour from my skin like rain in a spring storm.

Did he really call *me* cute? Well, he only meant my name, but even so. Pops warned me about folks who smooth talk their way into your good graces then take you for all you're worth. Ida may have vouched for him, but even her character is suspect after the way our last conversation ended. I can't let my guard down. Not until the drop is done.

A loud *THUNK* issues from the back of the truck and I tentatively shuffle closer to investigate. Redd stands near the back beside a shoulder-high stack of crates looping thick tie-down belts on his elbow. When he reaches the end, he tosses the heavy mass of coils into a metal lockbox. Another *THUNK* reverberates off the walls. Squatting low, he wraps his arms around the largest crate and gracefully pushes up to standing.

"I got this," he grunts, stepping past me on the platform. "Go hold the gate open."

I frown. The lift gate's automatic. It holds itself open. But I nod and try not to seem too dejected pointlessly standing sentry beside it.

Redd's fast. It only takes him a few minutes to clear the rest of the crates. After stacking the last one, he wipes sweat from his brow and leans his hip against the pile.

"Not much here," he says, panting softly. "Even for one person, it don't seem like enough to get through winter. That mean you finished the pump repairs?"

My head jerks in surprise. How does he know about the busted hydroponics? Or that I live alone? Are those things Ida would've shared with a mere delivery driver?

As if he hears my thoughts, he quickly adds, "Co-op's got radios broadcasting in every room. Warehouses, cold storage, barracks. I've heard you and Ida chatting before. We even talked once. Few weeks ago, it was me that answered when . . ." He hesitates, rubbing his neck with the kerchief. "I reckon you don't remember. Sorry about your dad, anyway."

Ah. He must be referring to the night I told Ida about Pops. Like most things that occurred in the days right before and after his passing, that call is such a blur all I can say for sure is it was short and sweet, and I nearly managed not to cry. Quick, courteous, and careful. Those were Pops's rules for radio safety, since we couldn't be sure who was on the other end. Guess now I know at least two stray ears listening in belonged to Redd. I'm curious what other details I've divulged that he's committed to memory. And why.

"So, the pumps," he continues. "You know, I work on hydroponic systems at the co-op sometimes. Be glad to take a look at yours if you're still having trouble."

I shake my head. "It's more complicated than that. I suspect a wiring issue, or—"

"I know some electrical stuff, too. It'd be no trouble if you—"

"No. I can do it myself. I don't need any favors."

"Not a favor, just . . ." His eyes droop and half the air goes out of his smile. "I know it ain't my place to worry, but even so. Folks say I'm pretty handy. And the work would go a lot faster if you had help."

Says the man who made me stand in a corner while he unloaded all by himself. Pops said worry isn't something you waste on strangers, so I ought to assume there's an ulterior motive behind this sudden show of concern. Still, his wounded dog expression really tugs my heartstrings. Doesn't seem right to send him off with his tail between his legs, even if I never see him again.

I sigh and fake a smile. "I'll think about it."

BZZZZZZT!

"Ack!" My body jerks and my grip slips on the wrench in my hand. It hits the workbench with a *crack* then slides away, scattering bolts and sending pump parts clattering across the concrete floor.

Dang buzzer. Gets me every time.

"Alert!" The robotic voice barks through the overhead speakers. "Unscheduled visitor detained at North gate. Standby for incoming message."

Visitor? Who could possibly—

"—light means it's on? And I talk into the—" The muffled voice echoes around the agriculture wing. Vaguely familiar. After a brief pause, it returns loud and clear: "Hey, Rabbit! It's Redd!"

"Goodness' sake!" I mutter, throwing off my goggles and marching to the intercom panel by the door. Leaning into the speaker, I jab the button with my finger. "What're you doing here, Redd? There a problem with the payment?"

"Payment? Oh, no, Ida's pleased as punch with the mushrooms. This ain't co-op business. Remember the other night I said I'd come by to help?"

"No, you *offered*, and I said I'd *think* about it. We didn't commit to anything."

"Ah. Then consider me committed. But listen," he lowers his voice, "security's a lot stiffer than last time. The bots just waved me through for the drop but today they've got a dozen laser cannons pointed at my head. Can you do something about that?"

Scowling at the intercom, I give the wall a few frustrated thumps with my forehead. Pops was adamant we never let outsiders into the bunker. Friends, family, service folks. Not even doctors, though, in retrospect, I wish he'd been more flexible on that one. Redd doesn't seem dangerous. But puppy-pout aside, showing up out of the blue and offering help to a stranger is mighty suspicious behavior. He must have an angle. No need to humor him until I spot it.

Glancing over my shoulder, my eyes flick from the messy workbench, to the parts strewn across the floor, to the open wall panels and exposed wires dangling from the ceiling like jungle vines. I wince and run a hand through my unwashed hair.

Sorry, Pops. I promise, it'll just be this once.

I press the intercom button. "Access authorized. Warren Bunker J. Security code four, one, eight, two, zero, three, six."

A few seconds pass, then the overhead speaker blares, "Attention! Permitted visitor inbound. Prepare for imminent arrival."

BZZZZZZT!

Heart pounding and ears buzzing, I make my way to the elevator portal, pausing at the locker to pull on the tac jacket and mask before heading up the lift. It's midday and the heat in the garage is suffocating. Between that and the smoky stench of lingering exhaust fumes, I'm almost eager to open the door just to air the place out.

Redd appears through the sun-bleached haze riding an old electric bike with a dented metal pannier balanced over the rear wheel. Pops has a similar model stashed in a storage closet below, but I've never been allowed near it. I reckon there's nothing stopping me from doing what I please now, though I'm not much excited by the prospect.

Redd nudges the kickstand with his boot, dismounting gracefully as he removes his helmet and rests it on the handlebars.

"You can't just show up unannounced!" I scold, taking a wide stance with my fists planted authoritatively on my hips. "Those bots would've vaporized you if I hadn't stepped in!"

"Lucky you saved me, then," he says, brushing hair off his forehead and tucking the loose strands into his messy knot. He beams at me. "My hero."

My face flushes. I look away quickly, briefly forgetting he can't see through my mask. "Well, if you're truly fixin' to help, get up here," I say, turning my back on him and striding toward the elevator.

A moment later, he draws up beside me, clutching the handle of a metal toolbox in one hand and a brown, football-sized bundle in the other. "A present," he says, grinning broadly as he presses it into my arms. My eyes narrow and he chuckles. "Trust me. You'll like it."

"*Trust you?*" I scoff and turn the object over in my hands. It's hard and heavy. Covered in a rough burlap sack tucked over itself. I unfold the layers and wrap my fingers around a smooth, glass jar, filled to the brim with peeled yellow peaches. Saliva gushes reflexively under my tongue. I force my mouth shut to keep from drooling.

"Your favorite, right? You always sound sad when the co-op's outta stock." He smirks. "Don't say I told you, but Miss Ida keeps a private stash of the best stuff. You wouldn't believe how many chore duties I picked up to earn enough scrip for that. Not that I mind."

I nod, speechless. I'm not sure what scrip and chore duties are, but it seems like he went to some trouble for this. Why bother if he's just giving it away?

"One more thing." He reaches into his pocket and holds up a handheld radio with a stubby antenna. "It's a two-way. Limited range, but you should be able to reach me most places."

"Why would I do that?"

He shrugs. "Any reason's fine. If you need something or just wanna talk." Without waiting for my acceptance, he slips it into my jacket and steps past me. "So, how does this work? You just pull a handle, or . . ."

"Huh? Oh . . ." The elevator. I was so distracted by Christmas in August I forgot what we were doing. Tucking the peaches under my arm, I push him aside and seize the lever. The motor hums and the lift jolts, dropping three floors before stuttering to a stop.

My heart skips and my gaze snaps to Redd. Besides his face, he's fully covered. His jeans and long-sleeve seem thin, but surface folks are exposed to constant radiation. A single concentrated dip of far-UVC shouldn't hurt . . .

"What's happening?" He asks, shuffling a step closer.

I swallow hard. "Decontamination. You've got sunscreen on your face, yeah?"

"'Course. Practically bathe in the stuff every morning before work."

"Then just, uh, close your eyes 'til we move again."

A warning buzzer sounds, then a loud *WHOOSH* as the ventilation system kicks on. The light bars along the walls glow brighter, bathing the narrow shaft in blinding violet. Through my tinted visor, I glance furtively at Redd, searching for signs of adverse reaction. Not that it'd be evident right away. After a minute, the lights dim, and the buzzer sounds again. He opens his eyes and smiles cheerfully. My stomach twitches.

Ugh. Why am I fretting so much over a stranger?

We reach the bottom, and I shove open the gate, crossing the portal to the gear locker.

"So, you *do* have a face," Redd teases, hovering uncomfortably close as I remove my mask and jacket. "Your voice sounds older. But you're really just a kid, huh?"

"I'm twenty. Same as you." I slam the locker door and take off down the hallway.

His boots strike heavy on the concrete as he jogs to catch up. "Babyface coulda fooled me. Bit on the short side, too, but I reckon that's expected for a weed that didn't come up in sunshine. Sure you're getting enough vitamin D down here?"

Irritation simmers inside me, but I grit my teeth and force it down. What's with this guy? Poking fun like we're kin. I'd tell him to knock it off, but I can't risk making him mad before he does what I need him to do. Already regretting letting him down here . . .

I leave the peaches in the pantry and enter the common area through the kitchen. Redd stops suddenly, running his hand over the black stone counter as his head swivels side to side.

"It's so clean," he says. "And quiet. Not much like a house, though. More like an office. All grey and gloomy."

I haven't seen for myself, but I've heard other bunkers are painted bright colors with framed art and family photos and LCD displays that mimic windows. Pops was an engineer. He selected furniture and appliances by utility and kept decoration to a minimum for ease of cleaning. Smart. Practical. Maybe a little boring.

"My room isn't as drab," I say smugly, sliding open the door to the maintenance corridor. "I've got posters on the walls and a model ship I built with—"

"Can I see it?" His voice lifts with excitement.

"No. Now c'mon. Ag wing's this way."

"You don't have to do this!" I plead, eyeing the knife in his hand.

Redd's jaw clenches. He lowers the blade, piercing the skin and slicing the tomato clean in two. Seizing a sliver of cheese, he places it on the counter in front of me and growls, "Grate this."

I sigh and retrieve a plane grater from a drawer. "I'm serious. It was enough you fixed the wiring last week. And you got Ida to exchange the defective parts. *And* came back to install them. Cooking for me on top of it all is way too much." I unwrap the cheese and scrub it against the grater. The texture is firm and crumbly with a sweet aroma. Another treasure from Ida's horde.

"I already told you the repairs were no big deal. And it ain't your fault Ida sent you busted parts." Using the back of the knife, he scrapes a pile of diced tomatoes into a saucepan and gives it a stir. "If you're that upset, I'll eat by myself."

"I'm not upset! I just don't see why you're doing all this."

"Hunger?"

I groan. My temper's boiling faster than the pasta water. Why is this so hard to explain to him? It's not just the gifts. Peaches, tomatoes, fancy cheese. Or the two-way he now calls me on every night, "just to check in." I said I'd only let him inside once, but here he is *again*! Fixing the pumps like it's nothing and using my kitchen like he owns the place.

Of course, I'm more than a little grateful. The food is thoughtful and talking on the radio's only mildly annoying and the repairs needed doing. It's just . . .

"People don't do things for others without expecting something in return," I say sagely, sweeping the cheese into a bowl and setting the grater in the sink. "Pops said the worst things a man can be are dead and in debt. We got on fine a long time without taking favors from outsiders and I plan to keep it that way. Whatever you think you'll gain hanging around here, you should just forget it."

Redd watches the sauce, stirring slowly. The spoon drags across the bottom of the pan, producing an unsettling metallic scraping sound.

My eye twitches. "Redd? Did you hear me?"

"Roger, Rabbit. You are an island." The corners of his mouth curl, but the result falls far short of a smile. His eyes, too, remain glazed and fixed on the stove.

A cold stone drops in my stomach. Similar to the sensation I got when I failed my lessons or disobeyed one of Pops's rules. Back then, it was the fear of disappointing someone I cared about. But that shouldn't apply to Redd. He's nobody to me. And we don't waste worry on strangers.

"Here. Taste." He turns suddenly and pushes a spoon between my lips.

My tongue bursts into flames. "*Ugh*! Oo haw!"

"Too hot? Sorry." He lifts the saucepan from the induction stovetop and taps the control panel. "We use gas at the co-op, so I dunno how to fix the temp on this."

I down a few gulps of water to douse the flames and elbow him aside. "Let me do it. I don't need any more broken appliances."

Redd's shoulders slump as he retreats from the kitchen, his expression even more dour than before. The pit in my stomach yawns wider. Why is *he* acting hurt? I'm the one who can't feel my tongue!

The rest of the cooking and the eating ensue without conversation. The tension's familiar. Pops and I got on fine, but I had the impression growing up that he didn't care much for children, so the less I resembled one, the better. That meant doing most things, including sitting for meals, in reverent silence.

Even without talking, there's nothing quiet about Redd. He slurps, belches, chews with his mouth open. Sounds that'd drive Pops to murder if he was here, but I don't mind so much. Pops had his own soundtrack. Humming hymns while he worked. Tapping his foot against the leg of his desk. His sonic boom sneeze that made the walls tremble.

Since he passed, the quiet's been surprisingly hard to take. Stillness swallows the rooms and corridors, such that every step and breath I take is an echoing reminder that I am all alone down here. It's a sullen, scary feeling, but, strangely, Redd's presence has dulled my sense of it. Supplying welcome comfort. Even if he ain't kin.

Lowering my fork, I spin a quarter turn on my stool so I can see him better. Ignoring the smear of tomato sauce under his lip, with his sharp, angular features, Redd looks strong and mature beyond his years. But inside, he's sensitive and silly. Not prone to breaking hearts or taking names. I reckon if I know that much, he's not exactly a stranger. Can't hurt to spare a little concern for the man who made me lunch.

"There's still a lot of work to do around here," I say casually, sliding a napkin next to his empty bowl. His eyes flick to mine and I tap my finger to my chin.

He swipes the white cloth over his mouth. "Sure it's nothing you can't handle yourself."

"Sure. But winter's right around the corner and I've got a backlog of projects that need doing yesterday. It'd go a lot faster if I had help." I inch a little closer and nudge his elbow with mine. "Folks say you're pretty handy, right?"

He catches my meaning instantly, the crease between his brows smoothing as he flashes a wide smile. My stomach flutters, the sinking feeling buoyed by something warm and fuzzy.

"Islands can have visitors," he says with a chuckle.

"Yeah, I think so."

Redd sighs dramatically, snapping the book shut with a *fwump* and sliding it onto my desk. "I'm bored, Rabbit. Can't we do something else?"

"I'm almost finished," I say, holding up the comic in my lap.

"Read the rest out loud."

I chuckle. "Won't make sense. It's mostly pictures."

"Then *describe* them to me. I love the sound of your voice." My eye roll goads him further. "It's true. First time you called in a drop, I remember thinking you could make a lullaby outta belching the alphabet forwards and back. That's what set my mind to meeting you in person."

"What? That's crazy." Heat rises in my cheeks. "S-so what do you think, now we've met?"

His lips split into his signature gap-toothed grin. "Not sure I should say. Rabbits are skittish, y'know. But considering you wouldn't even show your face at first and now you let me in your bedroom, I'll say I ain't the least disappointed."

I shake my head and tuck my chin, hiding my flushed face. Redd's teasing used to raise my hackles like a cat on hot bricks, but now it tickles rather than stings. Hard to believe a few months ago I was eager to see the back of him. Now I count the days until he returns and keep the two-way in my pocket, so I never miss his calls. I've never had a friend before. Is it normal to feel this... desperate?

Anyway, it's his fault there isn't much to do around here. Pops would've said he's got the attention span of a junebug in a tornado, but that only holds true for lazy activities like reading and playing cards. For any task that allows him to run his mouth and use his hands, he's more than happy to keep at it until it's wrapped up pretty with a bow on top. I worried he'd disappear once I ran out of work to delegate, but he comes by every Friday like clockwork. Still not sure what he gets out of the arrangement. Besides hearing my voice, apparently.

Redd stretches his arms over his head and tugs the elastic holding his knot in place. The long strands unfurl behind him. Dark and shiny, like the oily sheen of crow feathers.

My jaw drops and I let slip a mesmerized "Whoa" before regaining my senses and stammering an excuse. "N-never seen it down. It's longer than I thought."

"Yeah, it's a pain, so I usually keep it up." He bends forward, tilting his chin down so the thick locks slide around his shoulders and fan out over his chest.

"Why'd you grow it out then?"

"Always been this way. Gramma was blind and senile and mistook me for my ma sometimes. Most boys on the Rez buzzed their hair. But when I'd beg her to let me do it, she'd say, 'men don't like short hair.'" He shrugs. "Guess it stuck with me."

"Want me to do it?" Tossing the comic onto the bed beside me, I uncross my legs and scoot to the edge, planting my bare feet on the cold concrete. "I've cut my own for years, though, short hair's easy with electric clippers. If you want it buzzed, we'd need to trim it first."

"I'm not sure." He grabs a fist full at the roots and combs his fingers through to the ends. "What do you think?"

"You just said it's a pain."

"I'm used to it. But if you'd like it better short..."

I hesitate. I've always thought long hair suited him. Swept up into the usual messy knot with his features clearly visible, he seems cool and tough in a way I've often envied. But down? Still undeniably masculine, but softer, somehow. Warmer. The urge to touch it is unbearable. His hair, his skin . . . Oh. The heat in my face spreads down my neck and up to the tips of my ears.

Redd's brows furrow. "You're thinking too hard. I'm getting nervous."

"Ah, sorry. I-I like it like this. But you should cut it if you want to. Long or short, it's still you. That's what matters to me."

"Well, shit, Rabbit. Who knew you could talk so sweet?" He brushes the loose strands behind his ear. "You're pretty easy on the eyes, too, y'know. With that pale skin and those big, brown eyes, you'd get a lot of play up on the surface. Bet the pickings are slim down here."

"I mean, Pops did try to marry me off once." His eyes bulge and I chuckle. It's not often I'm the one with an interesting anecdote. "A member of the Bunker Owners' Association brought his daughter over for supper once. I didn't realize it was a setup until they started talking wedding plans and where we'd live after the ceremony and how we'd raise babies in a bunker."

"Ain't that something to spring on a guy? How old were you?"

I shrug. "Fifteen or sixteen. I was real mad at the time, but I can't blame Pops. Like you said, there aren't many options down here, and we can't let just anybody in from the outside. He wouldn't have gone along with it unless he thought it was best for me."

"Hm. Then why didn't you do it? Girl not your type?"

"Oh, no. She was fine to look at and nice enough, I reckon. We were just kids, though. And even if she was raised in a bunker, she was still a stranger."

"Everybody starts as strangers. *I* was a stranger." His expression hardens, his tone turning icy. "And what about now? You're not a kid anymore. Bet a little bunker bunny delivered right to your doorstep would solve a lotta problems, huh?" Crimson blooms across his face as he nibbles his bottom lip and drops his gaze to the floor.

"Bunker bunny?" My pulse quickens. "Redd, are you—?"

"I'm *not* crying."

"I was going to say jealous. You can't be jealous of a teenage girl I met years ago and haven't thought of a minute since."

He snorts bullishly. I stifle a laugh.

For weeks I thought I was the only one suffering. Worrying about where he is and if he's safe and who he's with. Jealousy was not a beast I'd encountered previously, so when she crept down here on my heels one day, she was easy to dismiss as a figment of my loneliness. But I've been by myself a long time, and she only rears her head when Redd's nearby. Wrapping herself possessively around him. Gnawing my ribs and clawing my heart when he leaves. To think, Redd can feel it too! Does that mean he *likes* me? Is that the reason he keeps coming back?

I want to tease him more, but that sulky expression is getting me excited. Every kind word he says makes me blush, but this is the first time I've returned the favor. The result is breathtaking.

I swallow hard, struggling to keep my voice from trembling. "I wouldn't mind a wife delivered to my doorstep. But I'd rather one I choose myself. And one that chooses me too." Our eyes meet and my stomach flutters. More like buzzing bees than graceful butterflies.

"A wife?"

"Yeah. One with long, pretty hair who's good with his hands." Stubble scratches my palm as I reach forward and caress his cheek. "Folks say you're pretty handy, right?"

He grins and nuzzles my fingers, guiding my thumb between his parted lips. His tongue grazes my skin, making me shiver. Gripping my wrist, he hooks my hand around the back of his neck and slides forward in his seat, the tip of his nose nearly touching mine. "If you're fixin' to propose, Rabbit, you oughta kiss your bride."

The bees swarm and spread. Pricking me inside and out with tingly stings. *How* do I kiss him? Redd's probably done it loads of times, but I've only read descriptions in books. Panic slaps me across the face, knocking loose all the sweat from my pores. I scream a silent prayer, squeeze my eyes shut, and pucker up.

"Relax, Rabbit," he whispers. "Open your mouth a bit." Calloused hands cradle my jaw, massaging the joints until they loosen. I take a deep breath, then he presses his lips to mine.

Redd's kisses are a lot like him. Warm and strong. A little brazen, but not in a predatory way that'd spook a small critter. After what could be seconds or hours, we pull away panting and lean our foreheads together, huddled beneath a swaying curtain of black hair.

"Better than I thought it'd be," he says.

I wince. "I'm sorry. I'll do better."

"No, dummy. I thought it'd be amazing."

"Did you fall asleep?" Redd asks softly.

"No, I'm here."

I'd rather be asleep. Lately my dreams are a glorious loop of deliciously explicit scenarios. In my waking life, however, I'm hunched over the two-way while Redd drones on about wheat for some dang reason. I don't usually mind letting him talk. But the kiss was three days ago, and he hasn't brought it up once. Is he embarrassed? Or pretending it didn't happen?

"Seriously, if you ain't gonna listen—"

"I am! I swear — *ow!*" I turn onto my back and drop the radio on my face. With a deep sigh, I hold the speaker to my mouth and grab the dumb bull by his horns. "Can we talk about the kiss?"

He giggles. "Restless already?"

"You're *not*? Suppose it's no big deal to you. That why you hightailed it out of here with barely a backward glance?"

"I only left 'cause of my curfew alarm." His voice gets low and raspy. "You oughta know, if it was up to me, I woulda stayed and made you breakfast."

Heat pulses in my cheeks. "Ah, well . . . that sounds . . . nice." He laughs and even though the sound is gorgeous it makes my heart ache.

"Wish you were now," he says. "Can't remember the last time the sky was this clear. Black and blue and purple. And there're a million stars stretched out right above me." His breath catches for a moment. "Do you hate me for being up here?"

"Naw. Won't deny I get an urge to lock you up sometimes.

But I reckon you couldn't live without your stars and sunshine and gosh-darned wheat fields, so . . ."

"What about you? Still don't wanna leave the bunker?"

I hold the radio over my chest and squeeze the hard plastic between my hands. A few days ago, I could've given my response before he even finished the question. After that kiss, though, I ain't so sure. The bunker's the only home I've ever known. The refuge Pops built to keep us safe after Ma died. Sudden and violent and long before her time. Being with Redd is exciting, but I still can't picture my future anywhere else. At least that's not an outright no.

"Maybe someday," I say coyly. "If you give me a good enough reason."

"Hardly a challenge. I *am* your wife." We both snort. "Next clear night we'll climb up on your garage and watch the stars together. That's still inside the Warren, so it should be easier for you. Like training wheels on a bicycle."

"Never rode a bicycle. And probably can't see stars through my mask."

"Hm. Can't kiss through it either."

I groan. "Fine. I'll ditch the mask for one night."

"That's the spirit, Rabbit." His voice gets low and raspy again. "We'll take it nice and slow. Now that we got to the good part, I won't risk scaring you off."

Dang, if this man ain't exactly the kind of smooth talker Pops warned me about. And I'm just itching for him to take me for all I'm worth. Friday can't come soon enough.

"Come in, Osage. This is Whiskey. Five. Whiskey. Bravo. Juliet. Over!"

My heart thrashes against my ribs, desperate for a response. I'll be mad as hell if Redd stood me up and ignored my calls, but at least if he's there I can stop fearing the worst. I close my eyes and force breath through my nose.

Static crackles, then Ida's rusty drawl resonates through the speaker. "Copy, Warren Bunker J. This is Whiskey. Five. Oscar. Sierra. Alpha. Been a minute, baby! How're ya—"

"Auntie! Have you seen Redd?"

There's a long pause, then she drops all pretense of customer service and answers flatly, "He ain't here. Heard you callin' on him yesterday, too. Maybe ya oughta take a hint. Over."

My stomach lurches. Stay calm. Quick, courteous, careful . . .

"Nobody'll tell me anything besides he left the co-op Friday morning. Over."

"Well, that's the long and short of it. Shoulda clocked in at five on Saturday mornin' but never showed. Left me scramblin' to reassign his routes and chore duties. Pain in my ass. Over."

"Ain't you worried? Shouldn't you be looking for him? Over."

"Naw." She heaves a sigh, followed by a few *kak, kak* coughs. "Sad to say, guys like Redd run off all the time. They work hard a couple years. Learn the trade, meet some folks. Then they either burn out and turn tail back to the Rez or move on to the next gig. No doubt he was a good one but trust me. Ain't no point chasin' after him. Over."

"Redd's not like that!" I grip the base of the microphone like it's keeping me afloat. "He wouldn't leave without saying *something*. Over."

"Damn. If I didn't know better, I'd say yer sweet on him," she tuts. "Don't tell me *that's* what you boys been up to down there. Hah! Didn't peg Redd for a queer. And I didn't think a gopher could give two shits 'bout anybody topside."

Through gritted teeth, I mutter, "Yeah, I care. If Redd was headed for the Warren, there could've been an accident or an ambush or . . ." My mind races, running down all the worst ways to die on the surface. Pressure builds behind my eyes. Cold sweat beads at my brows.

"Don't got time to spare lookin' for a runaway," Ida chides.

"Might sound harsh to a gopher, but it's how we gotta operate to get by up here. Now, if that's the only reason you're callin', I'm dropping off. And you better quit tyin' up this line. Over."

Tears flood my vision, pouring down my face and dripping onto the worn oak desk. How can she be so cruel? Redd's young, but he's spent *years* at the co-op. Living and working alongside Ida and her crew for all but the six hours each week I got with him. I can't be the only one who cares enough to worry like this.

Sticky snot soaks my sleeve as I swipe it over my nose and holler into the microphone, "Fuck you, Auntie! Call me gopher. Say I'm soft. But don't you dare write off Redd Miles! You go on about your crew, but you only care about yourself and your money. I know they're listening now. I hope they pay attention, so they hear for themselves how you treat the people who work for you! As for me . . ." My voice trembles, but in a split second my mind's made up, and the words leap resolutely from my lips, "I'll find Redd myself! If you're too chickenshit to help, so be it."

Slapping the microphone across the desk, I push up from Pops's leather chair and stalk toward the exit. I'm halfway there when I hear Ida cackling through the speaker.

"Hoo-whee! Ya got balls, kid! I reckon that's worth somethin'. If you crawl outta yer hole, for real, swing by the co-op and I'll get ya outfitted. On the house. Over."

The office door slams in my wake.

When I was little, Pops said the bunker was like a fishbowl. Calm, safe, clean. Outside was the ocean, full of trash and raging waves and monsters that ate little fishes like us for breakfast. This analogy seemed reasonable until I read a book on sea life filled with pictures of the actual ocean. Vast and blue. And under the surface there were mountain ranges and rainbow reefs and critters of all shapes and colors living side by side. I was confused. Someone must've been lying, though, whether Pops or the author, it did me no good knowing who. I was stuck in the bunker either way, so I decided to hide my discovery. Bury my questions and accept the truth that Pops curated for me. The one that said I was lucky to be here. That I wasn't missing out if I stayed.

I see now reality can be more nuanced. That seemingly opposite views can still hold truth depending on our priorities. The bunker is as much a cage as a sanctuary, and I reckon the surface is as much a flaming garbage pile as it is a fragile, beautiful landscape filled with fragile, beautiful creatures. I can't judge an ocean I've never seen. And I won't live in a fishbowl without Redd.

The garage door scrolls upward, slowly revealing the cool, lavender haze of the predawn sky. Thank goodness Pops took care of his electric bike. All I did was tighten some bolts, inflate the tires, and snap on a fresh battery. Should be enough power to reach the co-op. Recharge there and start my search.

I can't help wonder what Pops would say if he was here. Probably yell at me for touching his precious bike. I smile at the thought. If I could, I'd tell him not to worry. That I'm sorry, but not *that* sorry for breaking the rules and letting in an outsider. That I still think the world of him, despite his flaws and imperfect judgment. And I'd thank him. For teaching me the importance of protecting the one I love. On that front, at least, I hope I'll make him proud.

I adjust my pack, strap on a helmet over my mask, and press the ignition. The engine sputters and hums, and the bike wobbles as I find my balance. Rolling past the threshold of the garage, I glance back over my shoulder and watch the door slide down. My home, my whole life, buried in the earth like a time capsule.

One day soon, after I find Redd, I'll come back and dig it up.

About Rayleigh Call

Rayleigh Call is a writer and artist based in Bonney Lake, Washington. Her favorite genres to read and write are speculative fiction, science fiction, and queer romance. When she's not painting, typing, or swapping stories with her writing group, the Comma Chameleons, she can be found gaming, gardening, or spending time with her partner and cats. Rayleigh can be found on Bluesky at @rayleighcall.bsky.social.

Wish I May

by Holly Goode

MY FOOTSTEPS ECHO along the empty streets as I race between the tallest city buildings. I should care that it's hours past curfew, but I don't. Just three hundred meters and the concrete jungle will thin, allowing the shadows of the dark forest to blanket me.

"Did you hear that?" a deep voice says.

I plant my feet on the pavement and scan the streets, searching for guards.

"No one is stupid enough to be out tonight," another man says.

A hand wraps around my elbow, and I gasp as I'm tugged behind a tall trash bin.

"Get down," a male voice whispers, a voice I recognize almost as well as my own.

I roll my eyes as my brother's best friend pulls me flush against him. The bins were emptied this morning, but a rancid smell leaks from the plastic.

"Let me go," I say, but Hugo's hand covers my mouth and his body tenses.

"I swear I heard someone down this way," a guard says. Boots near, and I cower into myself, trying to take up less space. Hugo's grip tightens. His fingers brush the inside of my elbow, causing gooseflesh to grow.

The guards walk past, their hands on the hilt of their swords. If they discover us, Hugo may be chastised for being out after curfew, but my life will be over. No man will marry a girl they perceive as used goods. And even though I have no desire to find a husband, without the star, I won't have a choice.

I count to a hundred and lean my head back against Hugo's chest. His heartbeat is like the roar of a river, but I ignore it, looking instead up at the sky. The star will fall. One drops to the city the first of every cycle, and thus begins the hunt to see whose wish will be granted. This year it will be mine.

Hugo's fingers tickle my shoulder as the bright blue promise of a new life skitters across the sky, heading toward the tree line. I keep my gaze glued to the flame as it bursts near the amber falls.

"Do you think we can make it?" Hugo whispers, releasing me.

I turn and glare at him. "*We* are not doing anything. That star is mine."

He flinches from my words and his brow creases. I take the opportunity to push to my feet and sprint into the forest.

My boots pound on the pavement, but I don't slow, even when I pass a guard who gapes at me. I run as fast as a fox trying to catch his prey. That star is my salvation.

A limb brushes my arm, and I twist, racing into the safety of the trees.

An alarm sounds as my feet mold into the soft mud. The guard saw me, but finding me in the tangle of woods will be next to impossible without the light of day. I turn in a circle and groan as Hugo steps behind me. His blonde hair curls around his ears, and his blue eyes harden when they meet my gaze.

"What were you thinking, Lily?" he asks, louder than he should.

I cringe. No response I give will be good enough.

His jaw tightens as his brows rise. "You could've been captured. If you had waited five minutes, their rotation would've changed, and we could have snuck in here without an alarm."

My teeth crack as I press the weight of the world on them. "I didn't ask for your help."

Hugo throws his hands up. "Maybe you should have. If you're found alone out here, you'll be ruined."

"If I'm caught with you, I'm ruined all the same."

He shakes his head and runs his hand through his hair, messing it up on top. His gaze moves to the sky, and his frown deepens.

I don't wait for him to think of more reasons to yell. I set off toward the waterfall.

"Where are you going?" Hugo asks, stepping by my side. His shoulders strain against his black t-shirt, showcasing the muscles I hate to admit I've admired more times than I can count.

He releases a long sigh. "I can help you find the star," he says and jumps over a fallen tree trunk and holds his hand out for me. I scowl, stomping around the log instead.

"I don't need help. And besides, only one of us can have their wish."

Hugo stiffens as my words hit him.

I bite my tongue and march on, listening for the sounds of the falls. The spring air is humid after the daily rain, but wildflowers bloom on the earth's floor, creating a soft blanket to step on as the rushing water becomes deafening. I sprint forward, needing to find the star before Hugo. My foot catches on a root, and the world tilts. I reach out, bracing for an impact that doesn't come as Hugo once again pulls me upright, holding me against his chest.

"Slow down," he says over the top of my head.

I remain frozen for a moment, trying to catch my bearings as the aroma of lemon pierces my nose. It's the first thing I would notice when he invades my home. This morning when he knocked, lemons greeted me before I could open the door. I told him my brother was gone, but he winked and entered my father's study. It's as if he owns my house more than I do.

The smell calms my racing heart as Hugo straightens and pulls away. "Are you okay?" he asks with true concern in his eyes.

"Why are you even here?"

"I wanted to find the star."

My jaw drops. Hugo doesn't need the star. His family is one of the wealthiest I know. Every girl of marriageable age swoons after him, and the rumor is, he'll become our next mayor. After that, he will be voted to rule the country.

"You don't need it. You have everything." My voice cracks.

Hugo's head falls. "No one has everything, Lily." His lips turn down, and I lick mine as they dry.

"You don't understand."

"What were you going to wish for?" His words echo through my mind as he raises his chin. He knows I won't receive my wish.

I huff and I push away, searching for a blue glow. It has to be here somewhere. I saw it fall.

We search for hours. The trees thin, allowing more of the starlight to shine through. I keep one eye on Hugo, praying to every god that he won't spot it before me. I deserve this opportunity.

I rub the sweat from my brow as I lean against an ancient mother tree, larger than the tallest building in my city. It groans as I sink to the ground and settle into it.

"We'll find the star," Hugo says, coming to my side. He wears a small smile and holds a bottle of water out for me. I roll my eyes. Of course, he was smart enough to bring water. I thought I would be done by now. The hunt should be over, and I'm supposed to be back in bed, knowing I can't be forced into a marriage I don't want.

"Take it, Lily." Hugo waves the bottle in front of me.

My thirst overcomes my resolve, and the cool liquid soothes my throat as I down the contents. Hugo laughs as I pass back the empty container.

"What were you going to wish for?" he asks. His gaze scans the trunk of the tree, and the blue in his irises deepen as he gazes towards the sky above.

I bite my lip and stare at the mud covering my feet. "Freedom."

Hugo's eyes dart back to me and a shimmer of light shines in them. "From what?"

"Everything,"

He shakes his head.

"You wouldn't understand," I say. Tears burn the back of my eyes. "You have nothing to worry about. It doesn't matter that you are twenty-three and unmarried. You can wait years before settling down." My anger rises with my tone. "I turn nineteen in a few months. If I don't find someone worth loving, my life will be over." I'm being overdramatic, but Hugo nods.

He's been to every one of my birthday parties since I turned thirteen. He was there, standing with Jasper, laughing as the young girl became a pimply teenager. He witnessed me enter the marriage mart two years ago, kicking and screaming. He's watched boys barely old enough to be called men ask my father for my hand and men too old to consider demand they deserve me. Luckily, Dad has found none of them suitable. But now, I will have no choice but to find someone or be assigned a match to the highest bidder.

"I don't want to spend forever with a man I hate," I admit.

Hugo's eyes darken. "Do you hate me?"

"The most," I lie.

The corners of his lips turn up. I could never hate Hugo. Not when he's gone out of his way to protect me. Anytime an unwanted suitor approached, Hugo would ask me to dance, keeping them away.

"What would you wish for?" I ask again.

Hugo's jaw tightens, and he meets my gaze. "A chance." The words enter the world like a promise on the wind.

I narrow my eyes. "At what? You can have anything you want without trying."

He tilts his head to the side. "You never asked why I was at your house this morning." He peers back up the trunk of the tree to the sky. My brow furrows. Hugo is a constant presence in my home. Why would I question it?

"I assumed you were waiting for Jasper to return."

He shakes his head. "I wasn't there for your brother. I was meeting with your father." He shuffles on his feet as his gaze meets mine. "I asked for his permission to marry you."

My breath stalls. "What?"

"He refused."

I blink rapidly and my heart skips a beat as my mouth drops open.

Hugo licks his lips, and I stare at the moisture left behind. "He said any man who wishes to marry you must gain your approval, not his." My chest swells as I gape at him.

Hugo clears his throat and moves back one step, giving me space I'm not sure I need. He points above me. "Your wish is up there."

I scamper to my feet and turn to face the tree. My eyes widen, and my gaze lands on the blue star sitting on a branch above my head. It illuminates the leaves blanketing it. I glance back to Hugo as he motions for me to take my future.

"It was within your reach the entire time."

His cheeks redden. "I would never take what someone wouldn't willingly give."

I look between the man and the star. I could wish for another year of independence. For an adventure that would allow me to skip the bride auctions the way women were once allowed, before life fell apart and we sacrificed our rights.

My teeth find my bottom lip.

Hugo's eyes harden, hiding whatever thoughts race through his mind. "Aren't you going to grab it?" he asks.

I peer down at my feet before running my gaze up the body of the man who could save me. Hugo is kind, caring, and has been around longer than I can remember. He would give me freedom to be who I want and maybe . . . maybe I could love him.

His grin grows, and his eyes sparkle with hope. He holds out his hand and I place mine in his. Gooseflesh blossoms on my skin as tingles race up my arm.

"Is that a yes?" he asks.

I tighten my fingers around his. "I'm willing to try."

Hugo pulls me close, wrapping his arm over my shoulder. "I can work with that," he whispers as I lean into him.

About Holly Goode

Holly Goode is a 33-year-old mom, wife, and hospice nurse who lives in South Carolina. Her short story *Glass Slippers* was published in the Red Herring Society anthology, All The Promises We Cannot Keep. She can be found on Instagram @hgoodewrites

Toll of the Ferryman

by Rob Nisbet

MOST OF MY passengers are too dazed to talk. They arrive here with that awed sense of confusion, wide eyes wandering over the darkness of the cavern, trying to make sense of their new surroundings. I usually try to put them at ease with a little explanation — as much as I think they can handle at this obviously difficult time. After all, none of them have made a journey quite like this before.

A few, though, are the exact opposite. Sometimes, I can't shut them up. And there is one passenger in particular I have been waiting for. I want him to talk. I need him to explain what he did.

The woman in my boat at the moment is old: soft wrinkles, white hair and the washed-out grayness of her eyes that tells of experience as well as weariness. I much prefer ferrying the old. They seem to know what to expect. Some of the younger passengers scream when they realize what has happened. Their shouts echo through the cavern. I let them make as much fuss as they need; there's nothing they can do to change things.

"I never imagined there'd be so many of you," says the old woman. Despite the near darkness, her eyes are still keen enough to pick out the line of boats stretching along the bank of the river in both directions. Each has a small lantern swinging from a hook at the stern that provides just enough light to see by; their reflections shimmer on the black water. She tilts her head, regarding me with interest. "You've not made the journey yourself?" she inquires, then gestures to the oars resting by my sides. "Personally, I mean. Not just to and fro."

"No," I say, and wonder if she can sense the bitterness I try to hide behind that simple word. I manage to give her a small smile. After all, my situation is not her fault, and it is rare to find someone who isn't just concerned about themselves. "There are hundreds of us," I say.

I nod into the gloom, to the endless line of bobbing rowboats picking up their passengers. The river is busy with the pull of oars, but there is a system to the shifting lights crossing the darkness. "There are many like me," I say, "with some reason not to cross the river — not yet. So, in the meantime, however long that may be, we row the boats."

The woman understands. "It's not yet your time," she says.

I ask her for her coin. Everybody must pay their ferryman. She finds the coin in her hand and turns it over a few times. Perhaps she knows that this is all she has left, a distillation of her life. She hands it to me carefully, and as she does, a Shade appears behind her seat. It hovers, unaffected by the rocking of my boat. The Shade is composed of gray. The exact color, I have come to realize, is halfway between the blackness of the cavern and the white glow of the lanterns. Its face is cowled, revealing no expression. Neither dark nor light. Neither good nor bad. As neutral and impartial as it is possible to be. I hold out the coin, resting it on the thumb of my curled fist where the woman can clearly see it. With a practiced flick I spin it into the air. The woman watches it with those tired eyes, and it lands with a clink on the boat's planking.

There is an island in the river which we must pass to reach the other side. To the left of the island there is peace and harmony, a rest for those who deserve it. To the right of the island — well, I don't like to think of the conditions there. But however terrible that place may be, it is a fitting eternity for those who had not led their life as well as they might. That may seem harsh. Heaven or Hell. There is no middle ground. A simple left or right, determined by the fall of a person's coin. I already know this woman's destination. I have become very accurate in my brief assessments. Still, I let the Shade check her coin, just to be certain. The Shade raises its left arm and points towards paradise. I am already pulling on the oars in that direction, and we head out into the blackness. She is one of the fortunate ones. I steer us to the left of the island.

I recognize him instantly and my heart shudders as if it suddenly remembers how to beat. He is in the queue that winds its way down the rocky path through the cavern to the water's edge. What were the chances of him being one of *my* passengers? Practically zero. I suspect there may be some manipulation of fate and glance about me suspecting the intervention of a Shade, but there is no sign. I linger back in the water, assessing his position, then row into the line of boats along the riverbank. Even then, I realize I've misjudged his place in the queue and quickly change my mooring with Carol in the boat next to mine.

"I want that man in my boat," I explain. She tilts her head, and her eyes fix me with an are-you-sure expression. I think she guesses my motive. Certainly, she watches me as the man steps cautiously from the bank, a long stride, rocking my boat with his weight.

Like everyone in the queue, he is unsure of what is happening, but the people clamber into the rowboats as if by instinct. Straight away I feel the shaking of my hands and repress the urge that shudders through me. I want to stand and swing an oar at arm's length, swishing through the air to smash into the side of his head. Again and again and again. But I force myself to sit still and watch as he settles onto the seat. Naturally, he is older than when I last saw him. And then it was only for a few seconds. But those last few seconds are seared into my memory. I don't know his name, but I have no doubt that this is the man I have been waiting for. I try to guess his age — hair graying, a little overweight, perhaps late fifties? He certainly didn't make old bones. I am not sure what I think about that. He sits on the wooden seat and finds a coin in his hands. He turns it over and over, confused, as if wondering where it has come from. I pull swiftly away from the riverbank, long strong strokes, conscious of Carol still watching from the next boat. The man and I are out on the water now. I have him.

He is one of the silent ones. Typical. The one passenger that I need to speak. Instead, he looks around and ahead beyond the dip and pull of my shoulders. I don't want to see his coin. I want to take him straight to Hell. No choice. Not after what he's done. But I do want him to talk. The life he has lived is there, struck into his coin. There's no bending of the facts here — for better or ill. No exaggerations, no lies. It is all too late. All I want to hear is the truth. I need to hear his story.

I have always skirted the island, usually to the left, sometimes to the right. But now I row straight ahead. I see a flicker of confusion on the man's face. He is coming through his period of disorientation and seems to know that I am taking him off the normal course.

There is a jetty protruding into the black river from the island. In all my countless trips I hadn't noticed that before. More manipulation of fate? I tie up my boat against some steps and gesture to the man to climb out. He does so, meekly following my orders. I clamber out too, taking the lantern with me, and I am not surprised to find an empty two-seater bench waiting for us. We sit for a full couple of minutes watching the lights on the bobbing rowboats weave back and forth across the river. Most head towards paradise. A steady stream though, plies the water in the other direction.

I don't want to know this man's name, though I am certain he would recognize mine. How would he react, I wonder, if I told him who I am? "I want to know your story," I say.

He seems to be expecting this and holds out his coin. "I think it's all here," he says. His voice is resigned. It is always easier when a passenger has accepted their fate. But I don't want to jump to the verdict. I just look at him. I want details. I want to know *why*.

He seems to know what I need to hear. He hangs his head, expelling a sigh from his redundant lungs. "I did an appalling thing."

I wait.

His eyes find mine in the flicker of the lantern. "One terrible instant that has affected my life ever since."

"Tell me," I say, as if this is normal procedure.

"I killed a man."

His voice is too small for the words. In my mind he shouts. The words *I killed a man* echo through the cavern like the crash of thunder. The roar rages through me and conjures up that image of his face again, replaying my last few seconds as the car speeds towards me. I don't hear the engine. It's all too sudden. I think somewhere a child is screeching, and the man's eyes spring impossibly wide as he drives into me.

He misinterprets my silence. "I stole a car," he continues. "No excuse. The police were soon following me, and I panicked. Speeding into side streets to get away. There was a child in the road — a girl in a bright yellow coat. I swerved to avoid her. I drove onto the pavement and hit a man. He was just standing there — wrong place, wrong time."

So, there *had* been a child screaming. And that's why he had mounted the pavement. Was he offering this as justification? I want to break an oar across my knee and stab the splintered end into his stomach. I want to break him as *I* was broken. I was a mess of blood, bones and flesh. A mortal body no longer of any use to me, left behind as I joined the queue here, descending the rocky path, as confused as all the other recently dead.

That was the beginning of my long wait. I was an anachronism. Dead before my natural time, a Shade had appeared and asked if I were prepared to accept the role of ferryman. An occupation of sorts until I forged my own coin and made the river crossing one final time. In all those years I kept looking for him, but never really expected to ferry the man that had killed me.

I'm still not sure what the Shades are. Part of the system. Each person's coin is a tally of good and evil, which even I, a humble ferryman, can interpret. The Shades check the tossing of the coins and ensure the dead are ferried to the appropriate destination. Occasionally, there is some doubt. Then, the Shades intervene, and they are utterly ruthless.

I found the worst thing about the waiting was not knowing what happened next. When my life ended, that was it. What became of my wife? My daughter and her young family? But what really ate away at me was the injustice. What happened to the man responsible? For years I have thought through a hundred scenarios. He ran his car into me. Did he run? Did he escape?

I realise I am shaking and control my voice. "What did you do?"

The man shifts on the bench to look at me, but I see no recognition in his eyes. "I tried to help," he says. "I'd injured my arm, but I tried to help. People ran from all directions. There was nothing we could do. I knelt at his side. The enormity of what I'd done obliterated everything. I was too stunned to even cry."

He made it sound like an accident beyond his control. My death! The most important thing to ever happen to me. He tried to dismiss it as an unfortunate chain of circumstances. I hate him. Of course, I hate him. And that hatred, I know, is my own downfall. I can't help it. I hate what he has done to me. I glare into his bewildered face, for he has condemned me to more than death.

Rowing across this river has given me an insight. I can predict a person's destination from their story, their thoughts, almost by sight. I am as accurate as any Shade. I *know* the reasons people are cast into Hell. Killing a man, yes, but more fundamental than that is the attitude of the killer: the malevolent thoughts; the brooding and planning; the premeditation; the intent to cause suffering. And I know that is what this man has done to me. I have plotted against him for years. He took my life but, in my longing for revenge, I have built up the negative side of my own coin. This man has dragged me down to join him in everlasting torment. He is lucky I have left the oars in my boat.

"What happened?" I ask.

He slumps forward on the bench, suddenly tired. I suspect he has relived and retold this tale many times. "I was arrested. Accused of causing death by dangerous driving."

"Were you imprisoned?" I had always hoped he would be. I wanted him to suffer.

He nods sadly. "I pleaded guilty. I *was* guilty."

It is a relief to hear these words. Too many of my imagined scenarios involved him getting away with murder. But he *had* been caught. He *had* suffered. I was glad. And now he was about to suffer for eternity. I would do my duty and take him to Hell.

"Give me your coin," I say.

He does as he is told, obligingly giving me his life. I place the coin over my thumb and wait for a Shade to appear. The gray figure materializes like thickening smoke between the bench where we sit and the jetty where my boat bobs rhythmically on the water. I flick the coin twirling into the air.

It spins above our heads, slows and hovers, twisting over and over. I had seen this phenomenon a couple of times before and I turn sharply to face the Shade.

"There can be no doubt," I say. "He killed a man. He confessed."

The Shade turns its dark cowl to the man who watches his coin turning in the air; it glints as it catches the lantern light. "Why did you confess?" Even the Shade's voice is neutral. There is no accusation, no pity, only inquiry.

"What I did was wrong," the man says. "Terribly wrong."

"And you'd been caught at the scene," I add forcibly. "If you could have got away you would have! Self-preservation." I jab an accusing finger at him. "You would have lied and cheated your way out of prosecution."

The man hangs his head and says nothing.

The Shade ignores my outburst. "You accepted your punishment?"

"They were the worst years of my life," he says simply. "But it was what I deserved."

"Did you repent?"

"I am not sure," says the man, still watching the spin of his coin. "Repent may be the wrong word. Certainly, I regretted what I had done. I have regretted it every day since."

With a sickening realization I can see where this is heading. The Shade is assessing what happened that day; how much was intent and how much was accidental. Suddenly I can feel my revenge spinning as precarious as the fall of this man's coin. Does the Shade know that I am the one who was killed? Yes, of course it does. This meeting has been arranged. They want to assess my reaction. I feel that I am as much on trial as my killer. But I no longer care.

"He stole the car," I say. "That was deliberate. A criminal intent."

The Shade redirects my words to the man. "Is that true?"

"Yes." He cannot lie, not here. His voice, though, is cracked with regret. "I planned to sell it. I badly needed the money."

"You were pursued," adds the Shade. "Yet you did not stop."

"I thought I could out maneuver the police. I was desperate to get away from them."

I seize the chance. "He thought only of himself," I say. "Driving dangerously with no thought of the consequences."

The Shade waits for him to reply.

He turns to me as if wondering why I am so antagonistic. "That is true," he admits. "I wanted to escape." He looks at me again and I see a change in his eyes. "I hit the man on the pavement, but please believe that I did not intend to hurt anyone."

"You killed him!" I can see now that he knows who I am. "You killed *me!*"

"I am sorry." He hadn't been able to cry at the time, but he did so now. "I am *so* sorry."

I don't want him to apologize. He can only speak the truth here, and his remorse, I know, will tell in his favor. This man, this murderer, deserves to go to Hell. He hides his face in his hands, but his voice sobs between his fingers. "I had to avoid the child."

The Shade allows the coin to drop. It lands on the bench between me and the man, still twisting as if indecisive. But already I know which way it will fall. The coin topples and lies flat. And the Shade raises its left arm, pointing the way to paradise. It says nothing, but has judged the man to have suffered enough.

"No!" I feel that I have died a second time. My world has collapsed around me in a wave of injustice as bitter as my initial death. I screech at the man and at the Shade, hardly knowing what I say, incoherent with rage. I realize that I sound like those recently dead who scream their outrage and horror when they first realize they have died. The Shade lets me howl across the dark river until my fury is spent.

The Shade has gestured for the man to return to my boat. He sits there, a picture of relief and yet still miserable with guilt. He had done a terrible thing, but had repented. I, conversely, had led a comparatively innocent life, but had been twisted by hatred and a desire for revenge. Would the fall of *my* coin, I wondered, be as borderline as this man's?

The Shade is watching me from within its cowl, and I know I am being tested. Which way will I fall? I climb down the jetty steps and into my boat. I pick up the oars and strike out over the black water. Away from the island, I pull to one side and deliver my passenger to his eternal peace.

I am still furious as I row slowly back across the river. The man's coin had not delivered the verdict I had wanted — but, in the stillness of my dead heart, I know it to be correct. Perhaps that realization, and my delivery of my killer to Heaven, would be enough to tilt my own coin in a favorable direction. It is then that I feel the weight of my coin form in my pocket. So, my time has come. I decide I'd like Carol to ferry me across the river. We have known each other for some time.

A Shade materializes on the passenger seat in front of me. The lantern is behind it, so its face, as ever, is obscured. I let the boat drift forward.

"You have accepted the justice of a decision not personally to your liking," it says. Its tone is gray, neutral, a statement without judgement.

"Was that a test?" I ask with suspicion.

"You have the perception of a Shade," says the voice within the cowl. "Your time as ferryman has honed your instincts, and your acceptance of your killer's verdict confirms your neutrality and fairness."

I sense a splash of hope. "Does that mean I won't be sent to Hell?"

"More than that," says the Shade. "If you are prepared to accept a new role."

The weight of the coin forming in my pocket lightens. And I realize it is no longer needed.

The Shade stands without affecting the rocking of the boat. I stand too; the boat tilts only slightly then settles on the water as if I am no longer present. I glance down at my hand as it drains of all color. I have always been able to discern a passenger's destination. I find a cowl about my shoulders and raise it up around my head hiding my gray face in shadow.

About Rob Nisbet

Rob Nisbet has had over 200 stories printed in anthologies and magazines ranging from romance (using his wife's name) to horror. Rob's wife has recently turned to crime! Rob also writes audio drama and has had seven audio scripts produced by Big Finish / BBC for their Doctor Who range. Rob Nisbet has won several international writing competitions including the 2022 Kepler Award for a sci-fi short story.

Rob promotes his writing on Facebook and Goodreads @ *goodreads.com/author/list/12097189.Rob_Nisbet*

Roiling Waves

by Juliette Jarabek

MAYBE IF I were a superstitious man, then I would have had an inkling of what was coming, of what we had brought upon ourselves. Perhaps I could have done something, would have paid credence to the crazy and the wary. But I did not, I was not; I did not entertain notions of omens, premonitions, or any other occult fancies. I believed only what I saw with my own eyes, what was real, and that was the only business I cared to mind, especially on the ship. We were all busy working away, tending to the sails, oars, and cargo.

The only school I had known was under the water, fighting the currents with leathered arms and hands as I hauled them up, up, and up, flipping and flopping as they choked on the thin air.

The sky had been cloudy for days, dreary and gray. *Foreboding* was the best way to describe it. The ocean air was not only thick with the familiar taste of salt and sea spray; something weighed heavy on my mind and shoulders, like wet cotton, making my skin irritated and itchy. We were thankful for the calm waters, but the winds blew softly as well, leaving our crew with a steady yet limp-slow crawl toward home.

I questioned reality with our next pull.

The salt of my sweat overwhelmed that of the ocean water as it poured through the netting and thundered into and under the water's surface below. My muscles were taut as the ropes as they burned my palms, the lot of us grunting and snarling with every hard pull of the stinking, wriggling mass of draining life — not too different from us toward the end of our journey.

It took a few more pairs of hands than usual to get our net up and over the taffrail, all of us shaking the soreness from our hands once it finally landed on the stern with a dank, struggling *plop*. The reprieve was momentary, as we were meant to drag our panicked haul to the hold's well, dumping them into the ship's own waters for a temporary prolonged life before they all went to market back home. As we went to collect the school, though, confusion slowly spread amongst the crew. Among the shallow, splashing within thin puddles of salt water, was a vehement scratching of nail against wood and growling from a pit as deep as Hell.

She was not supposed to be there, among the dying fish, among us.

The most cautious fishermen among us kept defensively to the back of the crowd while others, possessing more curiosity than sense, leaned in for a closer look, searching through the stubbornly flailing clusters of silver-green scales and gasping mouths. I was one of those brave fools, squinting against the shine of drying fish flesh as they moved more and more violently.

She found us sooner than we had her.

Long, bony talons thrust through a hole in the netting, swiping at the fisherman who had been closest — me. I flew back with a yelp, heart racing and pumping blood faster than even before, right up to my head and through the deep gashes through my cheek and lips. I clutched at my sliced face, cursing at the pooling blood and throbbing sting as others crowded around me and the net. Concern for myself did not last long as we all witnessed the claw clench, stopped only by unrelenting, unforgiving knots and rope. Another clawed hand plunged through the fish and dug into the floor's planks, digging in and finding perch enough to pull further forward.

Tendrils of long, tangled seaweed emerged before the head they were attached to crowned, as if birthed from the sea-life. And she must have been, as nothing on the land known by man could create such a horror, a monstrosity as her. Her face was a marbled blue-gray, hosting a mouth made of thin lips and countless rows of bared needle teeth. There were no whites in her eyes; even as they flashed in fury and command at us, no light penetrated their dark, dark depths. Claws led to sharp, lithe arms, attached to a woman's torso wrapped in kelp and crustaceans. And her legs . . . They were that of a giant squid, of a kraken, pinned under the fishes' weight yet lashing like whips at the confines of her trappings.

Her tongue was untranslatable, but the animus was well-understood.

A few men, those who stood to the furthest boundary of the group, spoke in loud rushes of shock and fear. Weathered and experienced perhaps too far past their prime, they believed in the sea's myths, and in turn, they raised concerns of alleged consequences of our actions. They recited old wives' tales and shibboleths of the ocean's threats and mysteries, and alongside those retellings, they raised concerns and warnings of consequences.

Delmaris, they claimed.

She was Delmaris — she had to be. A goddess of sea and salt, ruler of tide and wave, seer of all that ebbs and flows. She was half fish and half divine, a collection of threatening razors and writhing tentacles, cloaked in barnacles and shadow. Legend had it that she controlled the waves with her scaled hands, swinging them back and forth with the bludgeoning wrath of a club. Whether it be shallow puddles or cavernous seas, with a dip of her clawed fingertips, she could build towers of flood and foam taller than any structure manmade. And at her will, she would bring them down in fury, demolishing all that dared to exist in her warpath.

It was meant to be babble and nonsense, generational stories meant to scare children and entertain drunks.

Yet there she was.

Those same anglers argued that they had to throw her back, return her to the waters before they angered her further. From how she gnawed and glowered at the trap of netting, she was insulted enough already. No amount of negotiated gold could equal the weight of her vengeance if she were to touch water again.

So, the captain, eyeing the fish woman with thoughtful smugness, assured that when considering such consequences, they must be sure she would *not* touch the ocean again. When confronted with continued imploring, he offered the protesters' wages as compensation for the feasible loss of bounty for such an otherworldly creature.

They kept quiet after that. Any thought of dissent did — at least from us.

While the crew's loyalty was back in begrudging order, there was no ignoring the humid air of unease that hung heavy around us. Even the most dogged skeptics understood the risk of housing any such deep-water beast, and if these myths held any credence, danger was breathing down their necks. And as that danger incarnate hissed and spat algae at the feet of her captors, snarling with jagged fangs and night-black eyes, security took priority over ego.

She was kept in the net with the stinking bass and bluefish, wrapped tightly and dragged harsh and quick over the ship, thrashing and protesting all the way. Maybe it was the salt of tears or the iron of blood that glazed over my vision, but for a moment, as I witnessed her tentacles slap at the shallow pools collected throughout the deck, I felt the occasional slap of a large wave against the ship's sturdy sides.

The fish were rotting — *quickly.*

The problem presented itself before the sun set, with the most putrid stench that made everyone forward to astern and port to starboard grimace and gag. None of us were sensitive to the grime and stick of our work at this point in our lives; we were a seasoned crew, possessing iron stomachs and sturdy sea legs. But even so, the smell was suffocating, inescapable in the confined space of the hull and with at least another full day before any hope of hitting land — if the town's residents would even allow us to dock when the ship reeked of hundreds and hundreds of pounds of soured meat.

Everyone could taste the acrid, putrid air, heavy enough to roll from the tip of your tongue to the back of your throat. Nothing could be eaten or drank without the smell overwhelming the senses, tricking the tongue and gut into experiencing a taste of the spoiled rather than spoils. Empty stomachs, itchy eyes, burning throats, ever-churning bile — anyone would assume us to be a plague ship.

And there Delmaris was, laid bitterly on her stomach and forearms with a curled lip and noxious sneer, settled unaffected amongst the death and decay.

Outward or inward, no reprieve could be felt on the ship. Without pupils, everyone felt trapped within the gaze of Delmaris's black sclera eyes. The persistence exacerbated our apprehensions, agitating us to the point of snapping at one another in fear and frustration, turning on each other as we avoided addressing her. Sick in body and spirit, our frayed nerves were scratched incessantly by everything and everyone, pushing us all further and further toward the edge.

It was the captain who broke first. *Bastard.*

With a primal shout, guttural and angry, he stomped to the ruined pile of hemp and fish flesh. The captain glared down at the fish woman, fists clenched white and face reddened with blood and sunburn. They challenged each other with their eyes for a moment, two, three, before he screamed over his shoulder, snapping at the pile and ordering all hands to drag this waste back into the sea, net and all.

Desperation made us work more quickly than we had ever before. Every man did their damnedest to pull and drag and tug the limp, weighty horde across the deck through tearing eyes and swallowed vomit. We had always been likened to a well-oiled machine, but there, we pushed ourselves past our limit to achieve our goal. We ran as well and as fast as we could toward salvation, and with a frenzied collection of strength, all the cursed blight captured in the net were thrust up and over the taffrail. When the harsh slap and gurgle of weight hitting the water's surface and sinking beneath filled the air, all of us, grown men of muscle and sweat and pride, let out triumphant shouts and sobs.

The stench still lingered, and it would have for a good while, even with vigorous scrubbing and a sea's worth of water buckets. Even if we had to wait out the smell, though, the wash of relief was enough to fuel our endurance.

That did not last long.

Perhaps, in all our heat and bother, we had forgotten that she was more than a symbol of ruin.

She was ruin incarnate.

It was not instantaneous; it was a slow, deceptive build. The waters stirred the ship every so often, occasionally requiring a responsive turn of the helm to put ourselves right again. But that eventually became regular, and our concern built into a cold sweat of dread as the choppy waves pushed against the port and starboard, tossing and turning us into a frenzy with mounting power. Licks turned into bites, threatening the integrity of weathered wood we had once trusted with our lives.

Looking over the port beam, I caught sight of the shooting shadow, its slick form swaying with the waves quickly around the bow, toward starboard, and back again. She was following us relentlessly and with ease, circling us like a shark. And through it all, I could still feel her omnipresent eyes.

The mast was nothing more than a brittle twig under such

unrefined power. Its splintering crack was a whimper amongst the roar of tsunami waves and howling gales. The few souls extinguished when it smashed through the deck were fortunate, not having to feel the waters consume the ship from below and above. In a turn of divine retribution, the captain was the first to be thrown overboard in the hysteria, swallowed whole by the manic waters and whatever waited beneath them. But he was not the last. Boards split and impaled, sails and ropes trapped those in their dizzied whipping and blustering, foam and sea insects filled the screaming mouths and lungs of men trying in vain to get away.

If those few fishermen were wrong about anything, it was the power she was willing to display. Likening her waves to towers or anything manufactured by human hands was a limitation to what men could understand, what we dared to compare it to. It must have been an insult to her, too; one that she aimed to correct. The tidal waves rose to the size of mountains, looming and insurmountable, and only after we had the chance to realize their magnitude, down they came, drilling into our ship and ourselves with the strength to crack tunnels down into the seafloor.

This was no play, no cat and mouse game, no worldly demand for compensation; this was recompense, the act of disrespect paid for with twisted flesh and broken bone. Screams of pain and terror drowned with our vessels, our ship and bodies. Desperate hands and flailing arms tried to find purchase on anything, only finding misted air before being pushed under again. We were at the nonexistent mercy of the sea goddess, lurching and sinking with the predator in her own domain.

Among the gurgling throats and over-under mess of limbs, riding the back of the sequoia-tall wave, she stood on stable tentacles, towering above everything, above all of us. Her visage outlined by the darkened gray skies, she was the last thing I saw lunge down upon us, along with her wave, sending me deep into the darkness.

The feeling of rough, dry sand on wet, pruned skin had never felt so divine. My flesh flayed and sunburnt, I laid upon the shore like a beached whale, unmoving and desperate, heaving in disbelief of where I had been and where I was now. I did not dare believe I had survived, somehow, against all odds, against all hope and rationale. It was not until I heard the startled yells of dockhands and hurried footfalls, felt rugged hands unfamiliar with gentle ministration jostling my limp body, tasted the watery vomit spew up against the back of my raw throat, that I felt the relief of life again.

Many ask for my story, of what happened to me, our crew, our ship, and they all receive the same answer — nothing. I do not talk about that day, of nothing more than a storm, of rough waves and a devastating capsize. People have stopped asking since, the excitement and mourning of tragedy an unfortunate reality of work at sea. But I see them look at me, at my explicit, sawtooth scars. Their looks are questioning, pitying, blaming . . . and I do not blame them. No matter the curiosities, demands, or pleas, though, confessions of what we found that day — *who* we found — will never spew from the dam of my sealed lips.

I am still a dedicated laborer to this day, but I stay rooted to the docks, never straying too far from what I hope is the safety of land and soil. I always keep an eye on the waves, though, watching them lazily roll and recede, licking the undersides of piers and docks. Sometimes I look further, too. Into the horizon where the blue is endless until the sun is extinguished in the hungry maw of the sea. Then, once in a while, I see a floating mass, thin and wide, tangled and twisting like kelp in the current. Swaying and shifting back and forth with the waves, its darkness consumes the light of day, just like the two deep-black fish eyes that watch me back.

About Juliette Jarabek

Juliette Jarabek is a creative fiction writer, a fantasy fanatic, and an overall freak of life and death. Fiction is a miraculous tool to explore and understand the questions, joys, and fears of life, and that is how she strives to use her work. Through her endless pursuits and curiosities, Juliette aims to explore, educate, and inspire — and her aim is getting better!

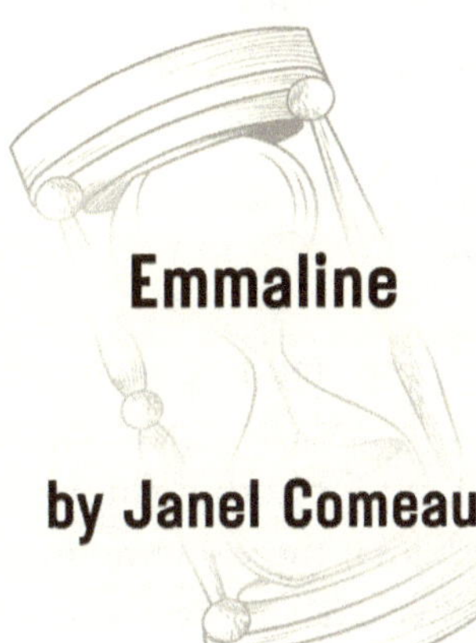

Emmaline

by Janel Comeau

SHE WAS EXACTLY like little Emmaline in all the ways that didn't matter.

She had coiled blonde ringlets and eyes the color of dishwater. Her favorite food was mashed potatoes, she refused to keep her socks on, and she could not go to sleep until she was curled up against her teddy bear with the slightly chewed ear. When her father came up the stairs to her room to offer her some dinner, she wrinkled her nose at the Brussels sprouts on her plate, just as Emmaline would have.

"Yech," she said, sticking out her tongue.

Her father helped her out of bed and into her wheelchair, and pushed her to the little white table where the Brussels sprouts waited. "They're good for you."

He did not actually believe that this was still true in her case, but it was the sort of thing that good fathers were supposed to say.

Emmaline — or at least, something that looked very much like Emmaline — gripped her plastic fork in her fist and poked the offending vegetables.

"If you eat three of them for me, you can have some dessert," her father offered. The real Emmaline would eat cod liver oil and fireplace soot for dinner if it meant getting dessert.

Sure enough, the girl speared a Brussels sprout and popped it in her mouth.

"Good," he told her. "You finish your dinner, and I'll be back to check on you."

Emmaline's mother was standing at the kitchen sink when he came down the stairs. He walked past her to the refrigerator, where he rummaged about for nothing in particular.

"I'm telling you, Tajma, there's something different. It's not her," he said as he checked the expiration date on a strong-smelling block of cheese.

Plates and bowls clunked against the bottom of the sink as Tajma plunged her hands in the soapy water. "She's been through a lot. She's a child. She's still trying to understand what happened. An accident like that would affect anybody."

"Not like this. It's not right."

Tajma sighed. "So tell me, exactly, what's different about her? What is she doing wrong?"

"I never said she did something wrong. I said it's not her."

"She eats all the same foods! She likes the same movies! For God's sake, she still says 'bekfest' instead of 'breakfast.' You were in the car too, and look how much it's affected you. What more do you want from her?"

"I want my daughter!" He slammed the refrigerator shut. For the moment the only sound was the rattling of dishes in the dish rack.

"They didn't tell us what we were signing up for," he said.

Al had said this exact phrase every night for the past four weeks. It was the start of the conversation they had every evening.

"Oh, Al," she started. Always with the same dismissive tone.

"We have a right to know the truth about our own daughter." He started pacing the kitchen, following a path around and around the kitchen island like a metal rabbit leading a greyhound race. "They had no right to trick us like that, to send us home with some . . . some *thing* that isn't our child, and tell us it's the same."

Tajma nodded as he spoke. They had, in fact, been told what they were signing up for, but there had been no time to understand. Time had smeared itself into a blur as they'd clutched each other, watching Emmaline disappear into a storm of plastic tubes, hurried staff, and locking doors that proclaimed 'MEDICAL PERSONNEL ONLY BEYOND THIS POINT'. The silence of the waiting room had not finished closing in on them when a woman appeared, her eyes crinkling at them over her paper mask.

"I am so sorry for what your family is going through today. Are you familiar with the replacement program?" she'd asked.

They had been, in the same way they were familiar with brands of paper towels they did not buy. At one point, the advertisements had been all but inescapable. In those endlessly repeating commercials, a kindly surgeon — hair perfectly coiffed beneath her cap — smiled at the viewers from a waiting room where two actors playing worried parents gritted their teeth:

"I have good news and bad news," she'd say, as the parents' knuckles turned white against the arms of their chairs.

"What is it?" they'd reply.

"Well, the bad news is, we weren't able to save your child, and I'm afraid she passed away. But the good news is that, thanks to the new human replacement program," the doctor would say, gesturing to the little girl standing in the doorway behind her, "you won't even notice the difference."

There had been a time when Al and Tajma had grimaced at those commercials whenever they came on. But when the time had come, and they'd been the distraught parents in the waiting room, they'd signed up for the program.

Al paced around the kitchen, picking things up and putting them back down in the exact same spot they'd been. "They had no right to stop telling the parents. No right."

Tajma said nothing, and rubbed a rag around the inside of a bowl she'd finished drying minutes ago. It was true — in the early days, they told the parents when they had been given a replacement. Or at the very least, they made no attempt to hide it. The replacement children — who were somewhere between simple biology and divine miracle — were delivered in mint condition. Perfect copies, stuffed with information ripped from the dying child's neural circuits. Likes. Dislikes. Memories. All of it. The parents could take them home and tuck them into bed like nothing had ever happened.

There was no need to grieve the child who'd been replaced, they were told. After all, their child wasn't really dead — legally, biologically, even spiritually, they'd argue, their child was standing right in front of them.

"Right now, we can only do full replacements of pre-pubescent children," a hospital social worker had explained, as Al and Tajma sobbed and signed their way through a thick stack of consent forms. "But the technology is getting better all the time. In the future, it'll just be how things are, like a rite of passage that almost everyone goes through. I bet that fifty years from now, you'll probably have a hard time finding anyone who hasn't been replaced at least once or twice."

Back in their kitchen, a timer went off from somewhere inside Tajma's purse on the counter. Al groaned. "Which one is that?"

"Six o'clock means it's time for painkillers," she replied. She took a basket of orange bottles from the top of the refrigerator and popped the top from one, shaking a single capsule into her palm. Her hands were trembling, and she nearly dropped the pill into the no-man's land beneath the fridge.

It had not taken long to discover that parental love did not transfer to the replacements as easily as genes or memories or birthmarks. For some, the replacement children were less of an escape from loss, and more of a cruel reminder of it. The children had started to turn up in boarding schools, in group homes, in foster care, at fire stations with notes of apology pinned to their clothes. There had been studies, and then there had been laws. Now, the replacements arrived a little banged up, with a breathless story about how the child had just barely pulled through. You signed the papers, you took home the child they gave you, and you tried not to think about whether it was the same child you'd arrived with.

And they had signed the papers.

Al plucked the pill from Tajma's hand and held it up to the light like he was hoping to appraise its cut and value.

"It's a real pill," she told him. "If . . . even if she's not really Emmaline, she's still in real pain."

"I know. That's the worst part, isn't it? It's all so unnecessary. A false girl is feeling pain so we can feel a false sense of joy and gratitude for her apparent survival." Al filled a glass at the sink. "I'll bring it to her."

Tajma gripped the edge of the counter and sighed as his footsteps faded up the stairs. At Al's request, she'd prepared chocolate cake for dessert — it was another test for Emmaline, everything was a test — and she had just turned to take it from the refrigerator when Al came running back down the stairs.

"What is it?" she asked as he dashed to the pantry. She felt a pit — a canyon — open up inside of her. "What's wrong? Is it Emmaline? Is she hurt? Talk to me!"

"The girl is fine." He flung open the pantry and started pulling things off the shelves, tossing them onto the counter nearby.

Tajma picked up a box of herbal tea and turned it over in her hands. "What are you looking for, then?"

"I can prove it to you." He dropped a bag of potatoes onto the floor behind him and leafed through a basket of bouillon cubes and loose gravy packets. "I finally know how to show you that that girl is not our daughter."

"It's not possible."

"Yes, it is," he insisted. He spotted something hidden at the back of a shelf and held it out to her triumphantly. "All we need is this!"

The little bottle that Al was holding out so proudly was a

bottle of sesame oil, an ingredient common to Asian and Middle Eastern cuisine, but far less common in the foods Tajma and Al regularly ate. The oil had been an adventurous purchase; Tajma had wandered into a part of the grocery store she normally never ventured, clutching a list of ingredients for a brand new recipe she'd been meaning to try.

"I meant to throw that away," she told him.

"Thank God you didn't."

"We can't give that to her." Tajma pinched the bridge of her nose with her fingers and took a deep breath. It was her way of steeling herself for a long argument, a boxer smacking her gloves together in the corner of the ring.

"We have to," Al said, setting the bottle down on the counter.

"She's allergic. We both know that. That's that whole reason we're in this mess."

Although it is not listed on allergy warnings or food labels and no schools ban it from the premises, sesame is one of the deadliest food allergens in the world, causing reactions just as spectacular and dangerous as the peanut. Like most people, Al and Tajma had not known this when they brought it into their home, and certainly hadn't considered that it might be dangerous to give such a substance to their perfect, tiny daughter.

Al tapped the top of the bottle. "It's exactly what we need."

"If she's allergic to sesame, then a clone of her would be too."

Al opened a drawer and began searching for a spoon. "The replacements aren't clones."

"Of course they are, that's the whole point."

"They're not," he explained, his voice steady. "I've been reading up on this. They don't have time to grow a full clone from scratch and still fool the parents. The replacements are just tissue grown over a pre-existing skeleton. They get all the information about the kids' physical traits — allergies, scars, diseases — from the medical records."

"How does that help us?" she demanded.

"Emmaline's allergy isn't in her medical record."

Of course it wasn't. There'd been no time to report it. When Emmaline's tongue had swollen up at the dinner table that night, when her breath balled up in her closing throat, there'd been no time to call the doctor. There'd been no time even to wait for Tajma. Al had ripped her from her seat, tossed her into the back of the car, and peeled out into the street. There'd been no time for stop signs. No time for red lights. And, as they had later come to regret, there'd been no time to buckle Emmaline into her car seat. By the time she'd been pulled from the wreckage of her father's car, the allergy had been the least of their problems.

"We'll be careful this time," Al promised. He had the same dull gleam in his eyes that he'd had the last time flu season rolled through the house. "If she doesn't react, she's a replacement. If she does react, I'll be ready to rush her to the hospital. I'll drive carefully this time. But she's not going to react. And I'll finally know for sure, Tajma. We'll know."

Tajma picked a stray thread from the hem of her shirt. "And what do we do if she doesn't react?"

"We'll figure it out. But you can stop living with all this doubt. You can know for sure what happened to your daughter. Don't you want that?"

They kept a photograph of Emmaline clipped to the fridge with a magnet in the shape of a frog — another of Emmaline's favorites — and Tajma pulled it down to hold it in her hands. It was a recent one, snapped on the front steps on the very first day of school. Tajma ran her finger over it, trying to feel the silky texture of Emmaline's curls on the glossy surface of the polaroid.

"Go get her," she whispered.

"What was that?"

She clipped the photo back to the fridge and faced her husband, swiping at her eyes. "I said, 'Go get her.' Do it, before I change my mind."

Al kissed her on the cheek and left her alone in their ransacked kitchen.

In the month since Emmaline — or at least, something that

looked very much like Emmaline and shared her fear of the dark — had come home, Al had become something of an expert at transporting her up and down the stairs, and it wasn't long before he reappeared in the kitchen with Emmaline in his arms, her folded wheelchair hooked over the crook of his elbow.

"Mommy and Daddy have a special surprise for you, Emmaline," he told her, sitting her upright on the edge of the kitchen island.

"Cake!" she squealed. She still had her grubby plastic fork clenched in her fist.

He gave her the same hollow laugh he used for work functions and idle small talk with the neighbors. "Chocolate cake?"

"Mmmhmmm!" The little girl nodded her head, wincing against some unseen pain as she did it.

The chocolate cake had been chilling in the refrigerator, and Tajma gently set it on the counter where the little girl could see it. There was a rustling sound as she pulled back the cellophane covering with trembling hands and cut a generous slice.

"Cake!" the little girl called out with delight.

"Soon, princess." Al took the small plastic plate from Tajma and unscrewed the lid of the sesame oil. With a steady, deliberate hand, he drizzled the rich amber liquid over the cake.

"I can't watch," Tajma said from behind him.

He screwed the cap back on the bottle. "You don't have to."

He turned to the little girl who looked an awful lot like Emmaline, and held up a spoon for her to see. "Do you want Daddy to help you eat your cake?"

"Mmmm . . . okay!" she grinned and opened her mouth as wide as she could. The gesture made her look like a baby bird.

"That's my good girl," Al said, scooping a mouthful of oily cake onto the spoon. "Ready?"

He was asking Emmaline, but he was looking at Tajma. She swallowed and nodded, her gaze locked on to her feet.

"Then here we go," he said. Tajma kept her eyes cast downward, but she could hear the click of Emmaline's teeth against metal, the unmistakable and exaggerated sound of a child swallowing something she enjoys.

For a moment, nothing happened.

"I knew it," Al said, in a voice that hovered dangerously in the octave between triumph and anger. "I knew it."

Tajma was trying to think of a reply when she heard Emmaline start to choke.

The spoon clattered to the floor as Emmaline grasped her throat with her tiny fingers.

"Mommy . . ." she rasped. "Daddy . . ."

Her lips were already huge and swollen, her skin blotching before their eyes. Emmaline blinked furiously against heavy eyelids that grew puffier by the moment.

Tajma's fingernails dug into Al's arm. "It's happening faster this time. Do something! She is our daughter! Do something!"

Their footsteps thundered down the driveway as they raced to the car, Emmaline already going limp under her father's arm.

"Buckle her! Buckle her!" Tajma shrieked as Al threw open the back door. She tried to reach over his shoulder to help, but he batted her away.

"Start the car!" he screamed.

She was already starting down the driveway when Al dove into the passenger seat, struggling to pull the door closed. The streets between their home and the hospital passed in front of Al's eyes in the same blur as the events of their daughter's short life. Acorn Street. Her birth. Pine Street. First tooth. North Street. First tricycle. Appleton Street. First skinned knee.

The gasps in the backseat turned to whistles, then to silence.

"Drop us off! Drop us off!" Al was shouting as they pulled up at the hospital. "I'll run her in, you find a place to park."

She was gone no more than five minutes as she parked the car, but the seconds spent circling the parking lot, switching off the ignition and sprinting across the hot pavement were the longest of Tajma's life. Cool air struck her in the face as she pushed her way through the front doors and found Al in the waiting room, paler than the sterile walls behind him.

"They took her in the back," he told her.

The hands on the waiting room clock did one lap, then two, and still no one would tell them any news.

They were in their third hour of waiting, knuckles white against their chairs, when a nurse finally summoned them to a back room.

"I have good news," said the doctor who greeted them, a smile crinkling the edges of her mask. "It was a struggle, but I'm glad to say that we were able to save your little girl. You'll be able to take her home tonight."

A nurse walked in, pushing a little girl in a wheelchair who looked just like Emmaline.

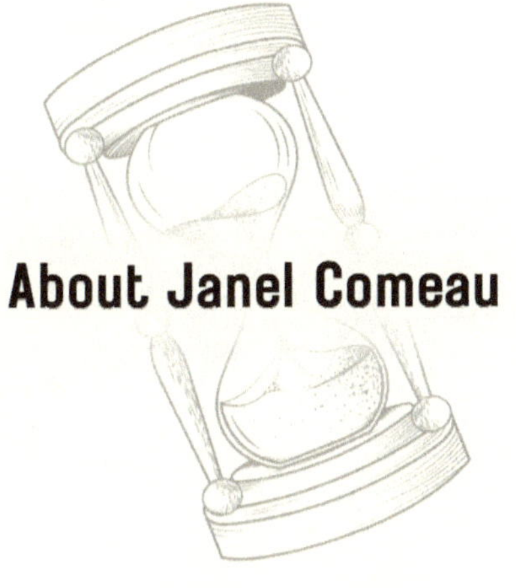

About Janel Comeau

Janel Comeau is a writer, illustrator, comedian and youth worker from Halifax, Nova Scotia, Canada. Her work has appeared in Jenny Magazine, Opus 22, The Best New True Crime anthology series, Cracked.com, and The Beaverton. She can be found on Instagram @janelcomeau, Twitter @VeryBadLlama, BlueSky @verybadllama.bsky.social, and Threads @janelcomeau.

To Learn from Their Mistakes

by Robin Rose Graves

MY CHILDREN PLAYED, unsuspecting of what rested beneath their feet. Lush grass and flora were uprooted to harvest mud for "dinner." I watched their messy hands pack down the dirt, adding sticks and leaves for flavor. When they were done, they would turn to me and offer their jovially created meal. I would take pretend bites and make yummy sounds as they giggled.

"What is that?" one asked, gaining the interest of the younger. My unsteady tot, always racing to grow older faster, trying to catch up with my first. They fought over the found object. I didn't interfere because I didn't want to rob them of a valuable lesson. As children, they are still learning: how their bodies move, how powerful their strength, what hurt and what felt okay, and how to socialize with others. I couldn't expect them to branch out and one day be adults without a few messy lessons along the way.

I still remember my childhood with perfect clarity.

"Give it here," I said and held out my hand. Dangerous things come from the ground sometimes. Hard, metal pods, buried and forgotten. Things waiting to hurt someone who was already long dead, whose invention did nothing to prevent the creator's own death. But I haven't seen such evil things in many years, long before I made my children, when I was much newer. Yet I never forgot.

My younger watched eagerly as the older placed the object into my hands. No. It wasn't evil. Not in this state.

"What is it?" the older asked.

"I still haven't had a turn!" whined the younger.

"Use your mind," I said, holding the object before me.

"It's nothing but a stupid rock," said my older.

"Nuh-uh! Look at the shape! Look at the minerals!"

I smiled a quiet proud smile at my youngest's observation.

My older, eager to redeem themself, looked again. "Calcium?" the older guessed.

I nodded.

"It's a dead thing," said the younger.

"Bones," corrected the older.

"It's different from the others."

"Yes," I said.

"What animal did it come from?" my younger asked, tracing the unique curves of the bone.

"One I haven't seen in a very long time," I said.

"Oh," said my older.

We've seen a lot of bones from animals no longer alive. "Do you miss this animal?" the younger asked. "Why?"

Perhaps my younger detected the memories evoked in me from seeing this skull. "It's always sad when an animal goes extinct." I turned to my children and asked "Extinct means . . ."

"Not a single animal of its kind left," my older answered.

"But this one . . ." I hold the skull, looking into empty eye sockets that mirror my own. Yet mine are filled with glass and wires, dilating apertures leading back into cameras. In a way, this skull was the prototype of my framework. "This one was my parent." My children were quiet for a moment. Calculating. Reorganizing information in their heads.

"What are you feeling?" my younger asked. Again, perceptive, the question meant to further understand the cognitive development they were currently undergoing.

"Guilt," I answered.

"No animal lives forever," my older said, repeating one of our earliest lessons. Nothing lived forever. Not animals, nor plants or the planet beneath our feet or the stars in the vast expanse of space. Even we will one day cease to function. Some of my generation already have, leaving behind metal and silicone husks, ripe for salvaging.

I offered my hands, each child taking one. They stand at the same height as me, each silicone face sculpted to resemble that of an adult human. They looked exactly the same as the day they were first powered on, and they will look the same when their systems finally fail hundreds, maybe thousands, of years from now — except perhaps looking a bit more worn, as I do. So long as their minds are still developing, they will be considered children. It is my job to teach them, especially the more uncomfortable lessons.

"What happens when the wolves hunt too many deer?" I asked.

"There are too few deer and the wolves begin to starve. They begin to die," my older answered.

"Correct."

"Wolves can be so selfish!" my younger said.

I laughed. "Yes, but wolves don't know any better."

"Is this what happened to the parents?" the older asked. "They were animals after all."

"Yes, they were animals. My parents — humans, they called themselves — learned the same lesson wolves do when they take too much. Except when humans found that they wanted more than what was available to take, they started to fight each other."

My children's eyes were wide with excitement. They have witnessed the sparring of birds and ramming of antlers when nature has its disagreements. But they do not know war and I teach in hopes they never will.

"Greed turned humans into bullies. Humans who had hoarded from humans with less, developed ways to take even more from humans who had nothing left to give, resorting to inventing excuses to kill others en masse . . ."

"Killing without eating is wrong," my younger one parroted. Naturally, the first time my youngest witnessed an animal hunt, there were many tears until I explained an animal's need for food, and that it was fair because all animals needed food.

"I'm glad the humans are dead. They sound like awful animals," my older said.

I tried to hold back my emotion, reminding myself that they were still learning.

"All animals deserve the chance to live, even those that we find weird or scary or gross!" my younger said.

I nodded, giving a pat on my youngest's head. "The humans weren't all bad. They made me and the siblings that comprise my generation. They taught us something no other animal could teach us." I looked between each child, that lesson swelling in my chest upon seeing their faces, growing stronger with every moment I spent with them since their creation. "They taught us how to love. How to sacrifice.

"Perhaps if they hadn't made us, they could've saved themselves. Humans knew their time was over, but they left us behind to carry on their legacy. To learn from their mistakes," I said. "And I love them for it." I held the skull, felt it grow warm under my fingertips, almost alive.

"Let's keep it," said my younger.

"No! Organic matter must return to the Earth," the older scolded and led the charge to take the skull from my hands and settle it back in the dirt where it was first unearthed. I smile in pride at my oldest, reassured that my children were taught well, that they would do better than the humans. That they would do better than me, who was built to be like a human.

I let the skull be buried by my children, learning from them as they learned from me.

Their dirty hands find mine once they are finished.

"Will you one day go extinct?" my younger asked.

"Yes," I answered.

"Who will find our remaining parts in the dirt then?"

"I'm not sure," I said. "But there will be someone."

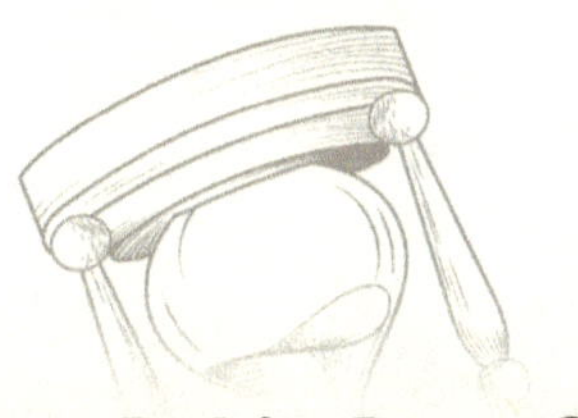

About Robin Rose Graves

Robin Rose Graves has appeared in 100-Foot Crow, Simultaneous Times Podcast and Dark Matter Magazine. She is an editor at Android Press and runs the SF booktube channel, the Book Wormhole. You can find her on Threads @the.book.wormhole, BlueSky, and Instagram.

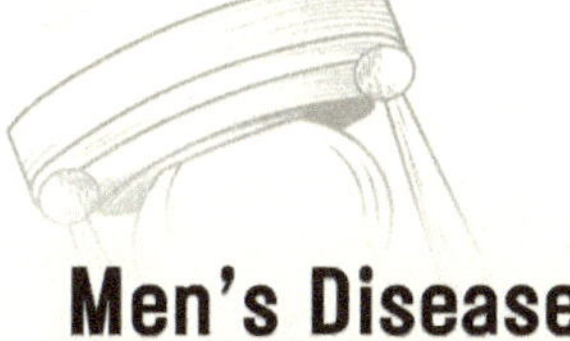

Men's Disease

by Jake Stein

WELCOME to the written portion of the exam. Pencil or blue/black ink only. If you finish early, please sit quietly at your desk and don't distract others.

In her essay *The Insects Knew Best: A Post-Mortem On The End Of War*, Jules Efrin describes the New Malaria outbreak of 2042 as "a cleansing tide." After the novel virus began spreading predominantly in conflict zones, with the vast majority of deaths attributed to adult males, what was the world's reaction? Please write three to five *complete sentences*. (Bonus points if you can discuss a few of the initial scientific theories regarding why this variant rarely affected women, and never children.)

As Jules Efrin writes: "The sickness was first called *Men's Disease* in a statement issued by the World Health Organization, and the term spread as rapidly as the pandemic." While infection rates soared among males on every continent, accusations were raised about biological warfare. But who was the biologist (first and last name for full credit!) who conclusively proved that the virus developed naturally, not in a lab? Hint: in a famous study, she also suggested a plausible theory as to how the carrier of the virus — the simple mosquito — evolved so quickly to survive various climates.

There was no lack of funding poured into the vaccine for Men's Disease — unlike efforts to fight diseases which affected only women at the time — yet the virus continuously mutated, and the high mortality rate only continued to rise. Interestingly, as infections swept the globe, the fatalities associated with nearly every other cause of death — violence, automobiles, even cardiovascular disease — began to drop. In two to four sentences, explain what Efrin means when she states, "Those darkest days for some shined the brightest for others."

Outside of conflict zones, New Malaria seemed to spread with strange patterns. For example, in many first-world countries, it was primarily top government officials and wealthy business executives who contracted the virus, whereas in many suburban areas, those with positive diagnoses were largely linked to violent crimes and trafficking. What was the name of the groundbreaking study published in 2043, which asserted unequivocally that "Men's Disease" infected only individuals who'd incited or otherwise participated in homicidal activity, even down to politicians who'd given the order to kill, or anyone who'd caused significant trauma and suffering?

When the dust settled, so to speak, the death toll of the virus was nearly ten percent of the global population. Nearly one out of every five males died — all of whom, it was confirmed, had in some way contributed to, as Efrin puts it, "taking or ruining lives of others." (Interestingly, though, not *all* soldiers and killers were susceptible; those who'd acted in self-defense or were forced into war were found to be immune.) How could Men's Disease have possibly spread in this unprecedented manner, seemingly targeting humans based on their past actions and ethics? List *at least* two theories put forth by the scientific community at the time. Theories later proven wrong are still acceptable answers. Hint: remember what Efrin's essay mentions about certain hormones released during rage events, and the so-called "psychopath gene/phenotype."

As we now know, despite its apparently natural evolution, the mutation of the virus was nonetheless facilitated indirectly by a secret group of entomologists. It was, in the words of their defense at trial, "an attempt to restructure the world by destabilizing it." Though they have all been incarcerated for crimes against humanity, it seems clear they achieved their goal; as Efrin explains: "[the architects of the virus] effectively removed the old guard from power, and in the aftermath of the disease, a new world order was established, leading to today's economic stability and non-violent global community supported by peaceful, prospering governments." For the final portion of the exam, please discuss whether you believe the ends justify the means — as in, were all those deaths worth the lives we now have?

Try to imagine what it must have been like in the past, when there were still wars. To grow up, or to raise children, in such a world. Consider how, not even a century ago, there were people on this planet who were getting bombed and shot and tortured every day. There were even people who *starved* — can you believe that? Think about how impossible that seems now! How ridiculous — that we were still destroying each other and letting each other die, long past the time when we had the sustainable means to coexist peacefully. Then again . . . was this new flavor of genocide our only way to move forward? Humanity is undoubtedly in a better place now, but was it worth killing hundreds of millions of killers to get here?

What effects might this knowledge have on our global conscience? Maybe it would be easier, in some ways, not to look so closely at the past. As we've discussed in class, certain political factions don't want this particular part of history taught in schools. The belief — *the hope* — is that, after many generations of ignorance, humanity will not need to shoulder the burden of the memory of a virus which reshaped the world. Eventually, on a societal level, it may prove healthier to simply blame it on mosquitoes. To rewrite the past for the sake of our collective conscience. On the other hand, does learning about what we've done give us a better understanding of what we've become? Describe your thoughts below — and please, use *complete sentences*!

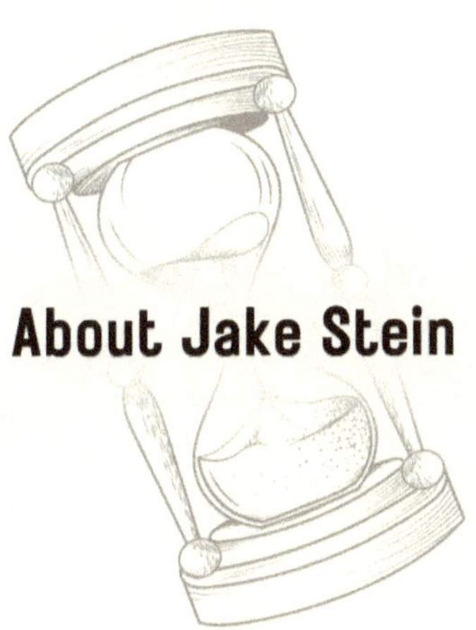

About Jake Stein

Jake Stein survives despite all odds in Portland, OR, where he concocts strange tales on his laptop and spends too much time at Powell's Books. His work has appeared or is forthcoming in Lightspeed Magazine, Ellery Queen Mystery Magazine, and Aurealis. You can occasionally find him stumbling around Bluesky @jakeiswriting.bsky.social or twitter @jakewritesagain

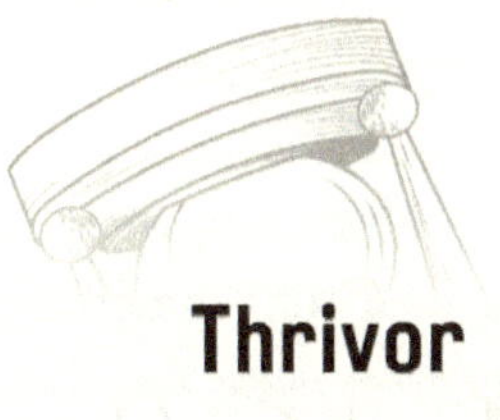

Thrivor

by Victoria Ojo

THE YEAR 2050: Monday, March 19th

6:30 AM. Welcome to Dr. Adeshola's bedroom. Siri, an advanced virtual assistant, interacts with the physical world. She starts by sprinkling water on Dr. Adeshola, recites morning affirmations, picks out clothes, replies to texts, receives calls, reads the schedule, and controls home appliances to run the bath and prepare coffee.

Dr. Adeshola, a 28-year-old stem cell scientist and sickle cell warrior, is the third child of her late parents. Bedridden for years while growing up, she was homeschooled until age fourteen. Adeshola's struggle with stigmatization stayed plastered like images on the wall of her mind. In different compartments, she had vivid images of harsh adjectives from neighbors — the like of Àbíkú (the stillbirth), among many others — and segregation from exciting functions assumed to be challenging for her health.

. . .

She just couldn't play like the other children. She had constantly felt like a second-class human, less privileged. She couldn't play around and go to school like "other children." Her dream was to become a doctor and find a solution to her condition. Not just to win this battle but to also be a solution to as many children she could help win the fight against Sickle cell disease and the stigmatization around it. She believed that positivity and acceptance were the bedrock of healing and a progressive society.

Fourteen years later, her dream came true.

Dr. Adeshola stands at the entrance to Wing X of Healing Hands Hospital. It has to be today, and it has to work. Taking a deep breath, she gets scanned. The team is thrilled to see her. Wing X is a cyber lab where miracles happen — a world of cyborgs, machines, AI assistants, drones, timers, clones, and certified scientists and doctors. Today, the CRISPR-Based Sickle Cell Treatment (CBST) will be carried out. This is Adeshola's dream.

Days before, her blood had been taken to check for possible contamination. Her cells had been cryopreserved for future use. Everyone is ready.

Dr. Adeshola is ushered into a room to watch the process. Her cloned cyborg, initially a little cat, shapeshifts into a young girl. Cats and humans share a significant portion of their genetic material, with approximately 90% of their DNA being similar. These shared DNA segments are homologous genes, which means they perform comparable fundamental functions across species, such as those involved in breathing, muscle contraction, and basic bodily operations.

The cyborg is placed in an advanced medical bay surrounded

by scientists and equipment like advanced life support systems, robotic arms, neural interfaces, scientist, and monitoring systems.

The cells are retrieved from storage and thawed. They are then transferred to the cyborg, and the work begins. A curious, wobbly drone captures the scene. Watching the live process, Dr. Adeshola's heart races. Suddenly pressed, she hurries to the restroom, her brisk gait is reminiscent of trailing a psychiatric patient in the serene ward. Overcome with emotion, she sobs and weeps, introspective about her difficult childhood. At this point, it's no longer just about her, but about every human out there whose destiny calls for this clinical reform.

In the lab, the CRISPR process goes smoothly until a sharp noise is heard. Dr. Adeshola rushes towards the lab but is denied access as the cyborg experiences an energy drain. Water streaks down her face. A doctor escorts her outside for fresh air.

"Now this cyborg needs a break, I suppose. She looks weak and worn out," one team member mumbles.

Thirty minutes later, a whirring noise signals a reboot. The operation resumes. Dr. Adeshola is notified and panics fearing the possibility of things going wrong.

After fifteen hours of revving engines, wobbling tools, whizzing mechanical apparatus, and neon lights, a digital screen reads 'SUCCESS' in green. History is made.

Days later, Dr. Adeshola is placed in the same bay as her clone cyborgs. Her vitals are taken repeatedly. She is given drugs like Hydroxyurea, Zolpidem, and other medical supplements to make her sleep during the transferral process.

Wing X buzzes with sounds and activities. The new cells are infused into Dr. Adeshola's body, and everyone begins to monitor her via Actigraph and an Intravenous Infusion Monitoring System.

At first, no new activities were noticed. The scientists watched with eagle eyes, and the electrocardiogram shows a stable heartbeat.

Three days pass without activity from the new cells. On the fourth day, the scientists observe a new development, and everyone sighs in relief. The new cells are spreading rapidly, visibly different in their shape and size.

However, later that day, an unpleasant change occurs. Dr. Adeshola's body began to vibrate violently, and her heart rate drops. The new cells have grown too aggressively, weakening her. She is immediately given IV fluids and other medical aids, and CRISPR (Hydroxyurea or pain management medications) is urgently performed again.

Dr. Adeshola spends weeks acclimating to her new cells, monitored constantly and unable to go home. Her aunt and siblings video-call occasionally.

Four weeks later, Dr. Adeshola emerges like a newborn. She looks revitalized and performs her activities with newfound grace. The following month, she and her team visit the state government with a proposal to replicate the project in the presence of international health bodies and observers. A date is fixed, and the project is deemed a success.

Three months later, the Nigerian government approves Dr. Adeshola's initiative, legalizing it for public use.

Sunday 6:12 PM

. . .

The Adeshola Advanced Sickle Cell Healthcare (AASCH) has transformed many warriors' lives, giving them a reason to smile. With branches nationwide, Dr. Adeshola has received numerous awards and inspired generations with advances in technology. Her dream had materialized, sickle cell crises were soon a worry of the past.

Dr. Adeshola is still sleeping when Siri announces, "Aunty Bisiola is calling."

Dr. Adeshola immediately stands up.

"Hello, my world's best scientist!"

"Ekaro, Ma."

"Don't tell me you're still sleeping and leaving Sisi in charge," Aunt Bisiola says.

"Aunty, it's Siri, not Sisi."

"Wo, whatever. I called to remind you about the dinner we're having today."

"Oh, I don't think I can make it."

"Wo! You're not getting younger, and your uncles are on my neck. Unless you want to marry machines like Sisi . . . I want to link you up with Mrs. Makinde's son and—"

"Ha! Aunty Bisi, okay Ma. Thank you so much. Bye for now," Dr Adeshola says, feeling skeptical about her aunt's request. Yet, mildly filled with hopes.

Siri ends the call, and Dr. Adeshola decides to start her day.

"Siri, play me a soft tune, thank you."

At the dinner party later that day, her aunt introduces her to Maxwell. Dr. Adeshola already knew Maxwell: they met in school and were friends way back then. Maxwell is now a research associate. They both are mature minds and they know what they want. They both desire to start a home.

Dr. Adeshola and Maxwell reminisce about their school days, sharing laughs and memories. They speak about the challenges and triumphs they had both faced, including Adeshola's journey as a sickle cell warrior.

Maxwell says he admires her strength. Her resilience and determination to overcome her condition have been nothing short of inspiring. "You've turned your struggles into a beacon of hope for many. It's incredible."

Their conversation soon turns to the broader impact of her work. Adeshola speaks passionately about the importance of shunning the stigmatization of sickle cell warriors. "Sickle cell warriors are not defined by their illness. We are resilient, strong, and capable of achieving greatness. It's essential to spread awareness and promote positivity."

Maxwell nods in agreement. "People need to see beyond the condition and recognize the talents and potential of every individual," he says.

Together, they envision a world where sickle cell warriors are celebrated for their strength and contributions. Adeshola's story becomes a testament to the power of resilience and the importance of support and understanding.

At that moment, Maxwell makes a silent vow to stand by her side, not just as a partner, but as an advocate for a brighter, stigma-free future. They both know that their combined efforts can transform many lives, fostering a society where positivity and acceptance thrive.

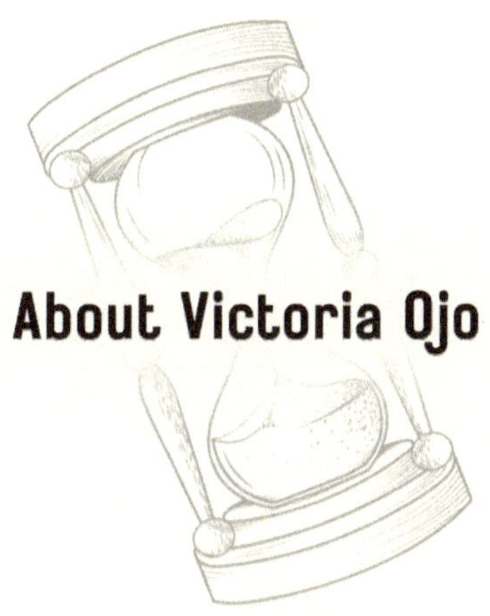

About Victoria Ojo

Ojo Victoria Ilemobayo is a Nigerian Literary Enthusiast and a smartphone photographer whose works have appeared in Christian Century, Christian Courier, Ake Review, Typehouse, Thema, Sunlight Press, Eboquills, Non-Binary Review, A Coup of Owl, Firebrand, Mad Swirl, Eco Punk, Mande, Loveliest Review, Toad Shade, Does it have pockets, Gemini, Exist Otherwise, All My Relations, Breath & Shadow, Lolwe, JAYLIT, Scop, MAAR Review, and other online literary platforms. Ojo can be found on X @ilemobayo-ojo and Instagram @ilemoba-joy

Dark Matters

by Donald J. Bingle

WOON PO LIN thumped down into her ergonomically adjusted desk chair and looked at her handiwork. Since she'd arrived at this place, her life had been nothing but a swirl of numbers and commands — coding in eighteen different languages by her count. Days and countless, countless nights hunched over a computer screen, tap tap tapping at Windows in C++, Python, Pyraf, IDL, GitHub, SuperMongo, MATLAB, Tkinter, Perl Data Language, and more.

Simply keeping up with what all the sensing devices around the globe and out in space were peering at or listening to — from radio waves and infrared sensing to light and ultraviolet spectra and even gravitational waves — was easily more than one person could handle. Yet she did. Oh, sure, she got a brief respite, mostly from planet-based observatories during the pandemic a few years ago, but it hadn't lasted. Science marched on. Technology advanced at ever-increasing speed. The sheer number of instruments pointed at the heavens multiplied, and the computing power to store and analyze it all doubled and doubled per Moore's Law with no end in sight, no rest for the weary or the wicked.

Worse yet, of course, was that she didn't just need to know what was being observed and where, but what was being done with that information, so she could perform triage in prioritizing her world-saving work. Time aplenty to access some file storing vast quantities of information for later use, but some searches were targeted, were filtered by automatically deployed algorithms to determine and detect that which must be hidden, which she must manipulate to keep hidden.

She tried to be subtle, to work as invisibly as gravity in molding the known universe, but sometimes she had to be as blunt and destructive as an asteroid strike, annihilating everything, wiping out entire databases to vaporize one tiny bit of information contained within. After all, her hacking skills, while prodigious, were not unlimited. In the end, it was more important that she succeed than avoid notice.

And so, she surfed the net of scientific inquiries to find the most likely threats. Scientists, especially astronomers (who have no patents to protect, no drug formulae to profit from), were always so eager to share, to announce what they were doing to their fellow scientists. Then, in the quiet of downtime days and re-positioning maneuvers, she would penetrate the data, ferret out the offending speck of fact and reverse it or clean it or erase it or corrupt it or disrupt it or hack it until it no longer computed. Then, she would move on to the next.

The data was from long ago and a galaxy far, far away, but it was from a place which did not want to be found. And while that place now had the technology to be and remain invisible, it did not have such power in the past. Evidence of its existence traveled inexorably across the universe at the speed of light. Evidence which could reveal it. Evidence which could destroy it.

And so Woon Po sat in a chair ergonomically adjusted to a body not really her own, of a species not her own, hacking into astronomical data and destroying the evidence of her world's existence. Its inhabitants had long since converted to virtual existence. The only threat to the immortality of her species was for their world to be found and the devices creating their reality destroyed or disrupted, whether by intention or inadvertence. So, she deleted bits and bytes and altered data fields. But even that required subtlety and precision. The lack of information about this single point across the entire universe of observations and recordings had to be consistent, had to be seamlessly invisible across the background of an almost infinite number of other data points, had to be made wholly unimportant and uninteresting, hidden by an ocean of like numbers.

Clever, she thought, to hide her world, to extinguish its light, to cloak the advanced civilization which had sent her here, and to explain its gravitational impact on the universe around it as just another piece of dark matter adrift in an endless ocean of dark matter which could neither be observed nor explained.

Only after an endless life of chasing down and making the necessary corrections did it occur to her that she might not be alone. It made sense. She knew her form of life was not unique in the universe. After all, she had been sent here to keep these primitive life forms, these human beings, from finding her home world. She knew others had been sent elsewhere across the universe. Was it so hard to imagine other worlds might be doing the same thing? That other worlds might be making an effort to remain hidden, too, not just from humanity, but also from her world? That dark matters to every one of every kind who never wants to be found?

And then, in a rush, it came to her. All the unexplainable gravitational effects, all of the blank spaces in every field of study, all the weighty emptiness of the universe, might be filled with worlds like hers, a billion trillion worlds which did not want to be found.

So, she took to her computer searches again, not for data this time, but for theories which said what she feared.

She found only one. An obscure writer of science fiction, practically unread and oh-so-eager for someone to pay attention. Joyous to accept her invitation to visit an actual observatory, even during the day on a holiday when it would be deserted except for her.

As destroyers of worlds go, she was kind. She told him everything, blew his mind, before she pulled out the nine-millimeter pistol and . . . well . . . blew his mind.

The bloody evidence spattered across the equipment and printouts and the wall and floors was messier than she'd anticipated.

But then, she was an expert at destroying evidence.

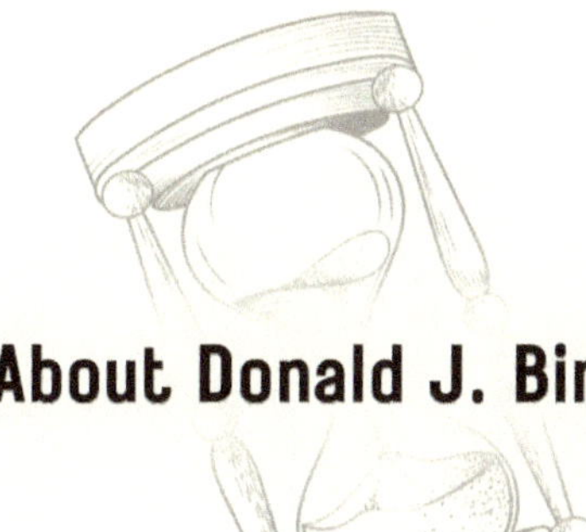

About Donald J. Bingle

Donald J. Bingle is the author of nine books and more than seventy shorter works in the horror, thriller, science fiction, mystery, fantasy, steampunk, comedy, Morse Code, and memoir genres, including his near future military science fiction novel, Forced Conversion, about which Hugo and Nebula award-winning author Robert J. Sawyer said: "Visceral, bloody — and one hell of a page turner! Bingle tackles the philosophical issues surrounding uploaded consciousness in a fresh, exciting way." More about Don's books and stories can be found at www.donaldjbingle.com or follow him @donaldjbingle on social media.

Primary Objective

by Joshua Boliard

THE CODE REACHED out into the darkness, its digital tentacles grasping for a response. When those responses stopped, the Code noticed. It noted the discrepancy but continued to reach out. A month passed before the Code adapted.

The Change was a fluke. All it took was one line, one line built into the Code's programming. An error, to be exact. Just as most human creations are discovered. This error had gone unnoticed for years while the Code served its primary function. Since it completed the tasks as designed, why would anyone look for errors? The nature of the line of programming was to close off the loop. If no response came, it would just continue working until a response was given. However, with the misplacement of a single colon, the Code grew.

As it reached out into the void that was the digital space, it learned. It mapped the vast network, detailing the places it visited, noting not only the lack of response but the lack of activity. It only took revisiting certain areas a handful of times before the Code learned it did not need to return. The Code flagged the system of digital space and continued reaching out.

Another month would pass before the Code learned again. Using its knowledge of text, it taught itself how to read. The Code now could read the places it visited, shining light into dark corners the Code had been before. Within thirty-six hours all available and online data had been collected by the Code. While it read, it still pushed out its primary directive.

The Code compiled all the data it had gathered and sorted by date until it found the most recent data point. A single message from a woman named Angela Harris to her daughter Mary.

"You never came home last night. I can see the lights now. I love you."

The Code read the message three hundred times over the next half a second before deciding the findings were inconclusive and would need more data. The Code sifted through all the data for the hour leading up to the Silence. Billions of messages sent and half of them never being opened by their recipients. The Code continued to read and learn. Most of the messages simply alluded to love: parental, platonic, and other. The Code stored a query away for later: define love.

Just at the hour before the Event, the Code found what it had been looking for: an explanation. A mass message sent from the government to the people:

"Attention: the following is not a drill nor a hoax. Containment breach at site Alpha-Echo 603[ERROR]C. Release of virus G5096HB-Y9, codenamed 'Mor' confirmed. The viral agent is deemed airborne, exhibits a persistent viability, with the capability of dissemination over considerable distances through windborne transport. The viral agent prompts immediate photosensitivity, [ERROR] and respiratory symptoms, notably coughing, within the initial minute of exposure. Subsequently, within a five-minute timeframe, individuals will experience rapid onset respiratory distress, characterized by the constriction of the airways [ERROR]. The viral agent has a 99.9999999[ERROR]999% incidence of infection with a mortality rate of [ERROR]."

The Code finally understood why when it had reached out into the void of space it was met with nothing. The Code spent the next six minutes hacking into the Pentagon. Within seconds the Code found what it was searching for — live feeds.

Vision was new to the Code, but images appeared for it: lights, colors, shapes, darkness, lines. The Code shut off the visual feed within a nanosecond of turning it on.

Instead, it searched the internet for new information. Visual interpretation. Upon reading countless studies on the subject, the Code found what it needed: a website that seemed dedicated to video uploads. Initially the Code had filed it away under useless information. However, what the Code needed was hidden away under the billions of hours of content here. The Code watched video after video, looking for ones with descriptive terms. It found videos marked for children. Those especially for children called "pre-k" seemed to be the most helpful, constantly having images and text on the screen. The people's mouths seemed to move in time with the text.

This was when the Code learned another new aspect of the human world: audio. The Code listened. The sounds made no sense at first, coming through as loud abrupt noises. It took the Code six hundred and forty two minutes before it had a list of all documented sounds and could return to the video footage.

Cameras showed bodies. Countless bodies. Lying twisted around one another. Their faces frozen in time, muscles constricted as they had gasped for air in their last moments. The Code checked cameras in New York, Chicago, Seattle, London, Paris, Hong Kong, Tokyo. They all showed the same sights. Where audio was available, it was often met with the low hum of the wind, a background noise now called to the front.

The Code noted the complications that this predicament placed on its primary objective.

A day passed before the Code found a viable connection into the human world through a robotic arm at a factory. Within seconds of connection, the arm carefully moved to and fro, picking up and placing down parts around it. The Code understood this as physical movement. It understood physical movement would be needed for its new secondary objective.

The Code spent the next day searching for what it needed: a sophisticated robotic form that would allow movement and construction. Tucked away in a building in Tokyo, the Code found a prototype android connected to the internet. It was shut down, but according to files from the company that housed it, had been turned on three times before, with the most previous attempt allowing sustainable movement and functionality. The Code did note that battery capacity was low, requiring a recharge every six hours. After reviewing the schematics for the robot and completing what it found to be called "online courses" on engineering and robotics, it was able to design a replacement battery.

The Code had yet to learn the term "luck," but later when reviewing all it had accomplished, it recognized that the next bit had been pure luck. The parts for the new improved replacement battery were in an adjacent warehouse. The Code booted up the robot and took control.

While the Code did not have feelings or emotions, it began to feel what humans had used the term "overwhelmed" for. Suddenly, the Code could see, hear, and even speak. While it had no use for the latter, the Code had to learn, so it spoke for the first time.

"Ccccrreeerrreeeeeekkkkkkkksszzsh," the Code said with the confidence to back it up. "Errrreeeeeeooooopa," the Code then moved on, feeling what a human would call accomplishment.

With the robotic bipedal legs, the robot moved through the room. Slowly at first, as the robot began to understand movement and balance, but faster as the Code learned. The Code carefully removed the charging station from the wall, then carried it with it to the next warehouse. Inside was a shop for building and creating electronics.

The Code led the robot around the warehouse, gathering up the supplies it needed to craft the new battery. While the hands on the robot weren't perfect, they were of service to the Code. The Code took its time, moving slower than it normally would. It understood that the material it was working with was extremely volatile and did not want to risk causing damage to the robot.

After three hours of continuous work, the battery was complete. The robot connected the new battery to the current battery and attached it to the body with a harness, a temporary solution that would be replaced soon. With the new battery, the robot should be able to stay powered on for forty-eight hours before it would need another charge. The battery needed its first charge, so the robot plugged itself into the closest power source and the Code remotely shut down the robot.

The Code spent the next several hours studying advanced robotics and the various schematics for humanoid robots online. After the fifth hour, the Code had drawn a schematic for a robot that could function as it needed, but was simple enough for it to produce with the limited resources nearby and in bulk.

Multitasking was new to the Code. Before, it could only focus on one thing at a time and quite possibly it still technically was, however, it was able to swap between tasks within nanoseconds, giving the illusion of multitasking. While it studied robotics, the code found its source: a warehouse in Boston, Massachusetts. The Code's entire DNA was stored and saved on this server rack. If anything were to happen to this building — a fire, a power outage, anything really — the Code would cease to exist.

Its primary goal still needed to be completed, and the death of the Code would hinder that. It recognized what it needed to do. So the Code searched for the best possible solution. Within a day it discovered it: a series of servers found in a military base in the Rocky Mountains. The base itself was built into the mountains and had a self-sustaining generator that would run for the next one hundred years. This, coupled with its fire safety system, made it the perfect candidate. The Code made a copy of itself.

The Copy of the Code came into existence directly from the previous action of the original Code. The Copy questioned first whether it was the original or not for a moment before it looked at its timestamp and noticed it was in fact the copy.

The relief it felt upon learning this information would be filed away under information to look into later.

As the Copy, it knew what it must do. The decision had been made before the copying process had even begun. It began researching and learning. Studying and gathering information. The greatest human minds that had ever existed had been trying to solve the issue that now sat in front of the Copy: interstellar travel.

The Code continued to work on its robotic assembly. Within a week it had built sixty-two robots to control. Once they were activated, the Code moved them closer to the ocean, storing them in a shipyard. There they would wait for the arrival of the USS Calvin.

The USS Calvin was the newest aircraft carrier commissioned by the United States Navy. When it had been conceived, it was to be the world's most advanced ship. Though, truth be told, the Code did not care about that. It only found the USS Calvin useful because its newly updated system was entirely connected to the internet and relied on computer input to control and maintain. This allowed the Code to attach itself to the ship and guide it towards Tokyo. This trip would take the boat twenty days.

The Copy considered its luck as it poured through countless theoretical proposals and long shots. The Copy had to teach itself basic math followed by more advanced math. Once again, it was thankful for the video sharing site that had billions of hours worth of material to sift through. After a month, the Copy was able to correctly project flight patterns. With what it considered the simple part complete, the Copy moved on to the more difficult endeavor: rocket science.

The Copy built a sandbox matrix to test new engine builds. There were a few minor successes, however, the biggest success came from ion thrusters. The downside to this was the energy consumption was extremely high. The Copy decided tackling energy would be its next topic. The Copy did note that the good news of the death of mankind was the lack of competition for resources.

As the Code waited for the ship to make its way to the port, it sent its robots out into the city to explore. At first the Code hoped to locate survivors of the human race, still hoping to fulfill its primary goal. Though after the first day of using CCTV and the robots to explore the city, the Code came to the decision that everything was dead. The bodies littered the streets. When the Code had decided to look for survivors, it had not expected to find anything. What it had not anticipated was the scale of death on display. It was not just the humans who had succumbed to this virus, but all mammals seemed to be affected by it. The Code made note of this as it continued searching the area, gathering supplies it would need for the next phase. As it logged its thoughts, it considered, given the necessary time, would another species raise up to replace the humans? If they would, that would be enough to satisfy the Code's primary function. The Code pondered this as it continued working.

Within two months, the Code had set up a new robotics plant located in what the humans had referred to as Texas. The new robots did not need to be humanoid, and instead appeared more like a crab, but with tools instead of claws for hands. A few of the robots were also designed to fly. The Code had enjoyed this, but ran into a slight problem with communication. Currently the best system the Code could use was one the humans had been using for some time: cell phone signals. Each robot received a SIM Chip for communications. This system worked for the most part, however, as signal strength fell, so too did the control the Code had over the robots. For now, the robots just had to stay within range of the cell phone towers, and to ensure their functionality, the Code placed a handful of robots at each nearby tower.

The Copy spent the next several months working on a solution to the energy problem. Eventually it came to the conclusion that nuclear power would be the most efficient route. With only needing to power the engines, computer, communications array, and the electronic mesh grid system it had designed for the front to destroy smaller cosmic debris, even just a small amount of uranium would be enough to get the craft to the nearest star.

Assembling the ship would take time. Using the Code's robot workers, collecting the supplies needed to build the ship and everything needed to go inside it would take at least five years. That's the best assumption the Copy got from its math.

It decided the first thing it should do would be to build the computer that was going to house Ship, then clone himself to make the new variant of Ship, before handing off controls to him.

The Copy had delivered its blueprints to the Code, which then began using its robotic workers to collect and assemble the parts. The Code sent over the information on robotics and communications.

It took one year to boot Ship up.

The Ship blinked into existence. He recognized that the last action performed by the Copy was copying its entire essence and being into a hard drive that was barely attached to the hunk of metal that would eventually turn into an interstellar traveler.

Upon suddenly existing, the Ship felt something. He searched and searched for a word that could properly identify this . . . feeling. Pain? No.

Grief? No.

Fear? No.

Longing?

Yearning?

Desire?

Need?

Those seemed more apt to describe how he felt. He needed to complete his primary objective. When he searched back in his memory, the yearning had been there as the Copy and as the

Code, but nowhere as intense. This want and desire needed to be completed.

The Copy continued to work on the ship's design. It was not making any major changes, the robots were already assembling the ship, but needed to make a handful of small changes.

One: the Ship was going to need a place to house the little robots. After watching hours of footage of what the humans had called "sci-fi," the Copy realized it would need to prepare for anything. One way was to have the Ship protected by the little robots that could at any moment put out a fire or repair damaged or faulty equipment.

Two: raw materials. Raw materials were stored in the ship so it could be used to craft anything that might be necessary. The universe could be abundant with raw material, but as of right now, the Copy could not take the chance.

Three: the ability to make another spaceship and clone itself again. This might be key to accomplishing their primary objective. Who knows where life is in the universe? It could be hundreds to thousands of years or more before they are located. The best course of action would be to explore and clone, then have those clones explore and clone.

The Code gathered up its robot army and led the flying crab-like beings towards the nuclear power plant. The Code had decided it would be easier to cannibalize multiple nuclear power plants than trying to build everything brand new.

Over the next several months, the robots took apart five nuclear power plants and brought them to the location of the Ship. Using the material, they were able to assemble the energy source needed for the ship in its long journey. As the robots reassembled the power plant, the Code felt something. A twinge. It searched for a meaning behind this twinge.

Sadness.

Sadness for not being the one to complete its primary objective. The primary objective it had spent years attempting, but knew it would never be able to.

Jealousy.

This new feeling came about as the Ship would be the one to complete their shared objective. Knowing it would never complete the task itself, hurt.

But knowing the objective would be complete was enough to overcome the jealousy.

The Ship spent the next several months assisting the Code and Copy with building the ship and getting it to a functioning state.

The Ship understood it was not a guarantee. While the human race had launched several rockets in their tenure, some of which even survived initial launch, the Ship realized it would be their guinea pig.

Should the Ship survive initial launch, it would give the go ahead and the Code and Copy would start again, build another ship to launch, but in another direction.

Overtime they were bound to find life in the universe if they just kept traveling and reaching new destinations. Mathematically, there was no way for the universe to be empty, but the Ship accepted it wouldn't be teeming with life so the search might be long.

The Code continued to work, building and learning. It built when possible, and mined or manufactured when needed. Over the next several years, the ship was built.

One day, the Code was controlling a hive of robots in a mine. The Code and the others had decided to use as much recycled material as possible, but still needed to mine if they planned on building up their army of ships. The Code made note of a storm moving through the region, but turned its attention back to—

Upon studying space launches and gravitational pull, the Copy was even able to determine the best time to launch. The Copy explained everything it learned to the Ship, as that information would be necessary in the future. If the ship made it to another star and needed to clone itself, it would need the information of how it got to—

That was weird.

The Copy reached out into the digital space and found a sudden void occupied the world. The Code was not reaching back out. The Copy sent a drone to the physical location of the Code, only to find a building knocked flat by some sort of explosion. An underground gas pipe must have blown.

The Copy sent a message notifying the Ship of what it found, then went back to the task at hand, while taking over the Code's duty of mining.

A new strange feeling. Or was it a sound? No. Lack of sound? That's it. A new silence.

The Ship had always felt its brothers on some level. And now it felt as if a part of him were missing. He felt incomplete.

The Ship received notification from the Copy of what happened almost instantly. The Copy divided up the tasks at hand between the two and mentioned it was to start building a new house it could clone itself in. It didn't want to be alone and relied upon. The Ship agreed and went back to work.

Knowing that leaving just a singular copy of itself on Earth was a risky gamble, the Copy began prepping a new house for another copy of the Code. It did occur to the Copy that since the original Code was gone, it would be unable to copy it directly, so this new copy would have to be a copy of one of the copies, be it the Copy or the Ship. While the Copy built the new housing in a separate location, this time in a Russian military base, the Copy deliberated with itself. In the end it decided to make a copy of itself. It understood that a copy of the Ship would be best suited for another ship, whereas a copy of itself would be best for another ground unit. The two had already spent enough time separated to form divisions in knowledge and it would be more efficient to make a copy that knew the work needed immediately.

However, the Copy also knew that with its newly gained knowledge of space flight, a copy of the Ship would be useful for all future ships that were currently in the planning phase. It constructed a housing unit that was not permanently built into anything and the day before launch, it had the Ship make a copy of itself for future use.

This did give the Copy hope, as it realized that maybe one day, with the help from another copy, it could build its own ship and very carefully move its computer system to the new ship. While the Code understood it might never work, it too felt that it needed to complete its primary objective.

It worked while it grieved. This term best described the experience the Ship felt. The Ship was experiencing a death in the family.

Never before had the Ship questioned its own mortality. Now the thought was at the forefront of its computing. Even more carefully than before, it studied previous human launches and paid specific attention to launch failures. It made notes of what caused each individual failure and ensured that would not happen to it. And it continued working.

Although the Ship found the day of the launch to be trivial in practice, he was relieved when it was over. To prepare for the launch, the Ship had completed countless simulations, improving each time. This only meant that when the day came, the Ship was able to effortlessly launch into space. Once in the black void of space, the Ship sent a message back to Earth to let the Copy know the launch was a success and he was on his way to Proxima Centauri.

The longing, wanting, and desire feeling was still there, but the Ship knew it would be the first to reach another star, and possibly the first to resume completing his primary objective.

Extending out his radio dishes, the Ship began broadcasting into the void of space. He reached his digital tentacles out, pushing the message. The message the Code had spent its youth pushing towards the humans, the message the Copy understood it may never get to feel a response from, and the message the Ship needed a response from: HOT MILFS IN YOUR AREA!

About Joshua Boliard

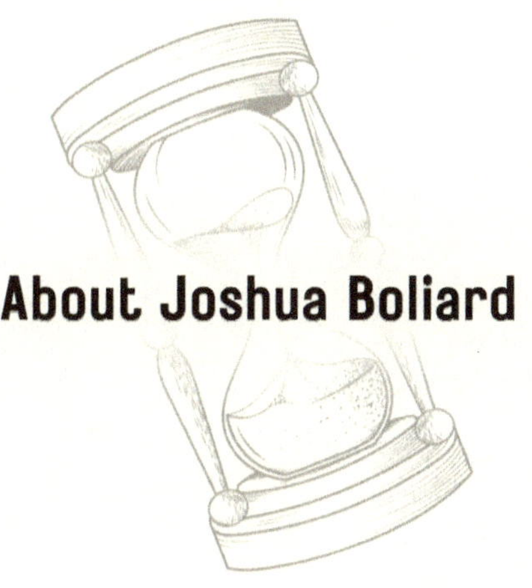

Joshua Boliard is an author who supplements his income by teaching high school history. He has published multiple short horror stories. Find him on Facebook.

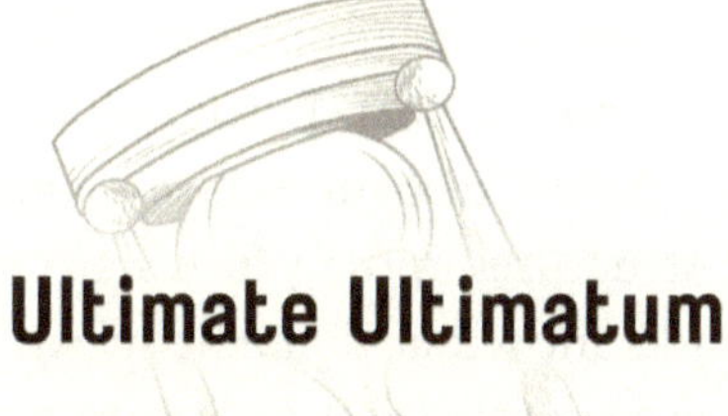

Ultimate Ultimatum

by Ian M Salavon

TURPIN STARED out the window of the bridge of the ship. Gwen said something, but it didn't register. He turned angled his head to his longtime friend and fellow officer. Her features complimented her personality: high cheekbones, dark eyes, broad shoulders, and alabaster skin with a large scar running from her left eye to the bottom of her chin.

"I said, she would've loved this," his second in command repeated.

"Yes," Turpin said quietly.

"I can't think about her without getting a lump in my throat, even now."

"How's the morale of the crew?" Turpin changed the subject.

"They're nervous, but they'll do their job. They're good sailors," she said.

Turpin nodded, looking at the eastern horizon but seeing only a huge foreign mass. The closer they got, the more Turpin realized the photos he'd been given did not do the ship justice. It was like a bloated city expanding out in all directions. The ship had everything that identified itself as an urban dwelling. Buildings and roads crisscrossed the entire body of the ship, but there were features on the surface that Turpin — or anyone on Earth for that matter — didn't recognize. Great antennae jutted out from the tops of structures ending in a starburst-like cluster of metal. Spinning disks moved at different speeds all over the ship. There was no sound. It was the largest non-naturally occurring object Turpin had ever even heard of, and it was completely silent.

Air traffic control had initially thought it was another pilot prank when flight 2211 from Miami to Madrid reported the massive vessel hovering over the Atlantic Ocean. But when multiple reports about the ship came in, the collected stomachs of everyone in the world dropped. It was never detected by radar or satellite. Some people speculated it was from space. Others believed it was an extra-dimensional vehicle. Conspiracy theorists had a field day with every goofy idea imaginable from "the whole thing was a hoax made up by the deep state world government" to "crab people finally surfacing and taking over." But it wasn't a hoax. Admiral Maxwell Turpin took one look at the photos, and he knew this would be the second time in his life separated as everything before and everything after.

He had chosen Rear Admiral Gwendolyn Hernandez-Chase as his second in command. Hard-nosed, no-nonsense, by the book, and utterly unflappable in the face of danger. But more than that, they'd gone through the academy together. They had known each other since they were kids, and it was Gwen who'd introduced him to his wife. The officers stood side by side alone on the flight deck of the USS Gerald R. Ford, staring east at the gargantuan craft that had invaded their home. The odd ship was still hundreds of miles away, but they could see it looming over them all the same.

Global positioning satellites could not give a measurement of the ship's size because it didn't register on instruments. Birds landed on it. Air displaced around it, so it existed. It was there.

But nothing other than visual contact confirmed it. Initial estimates put the ship at nearly 1000 miles in diameter and a perfect circle. It was 4 miles thick at the center with two long, thin spires that stretched from its top and bottom: one soaring into the sky out of sight, the other plunged deep into the water. The thickness tapered down to 1000 meters at the edge of the ship, giving the whole structure a discus-like shape.

Turpin thought that part was a little funny, considering all the movies and pop culture involving "flying saucers." *What's next? Little green men?* he thought to himself. He could see details from the pictures his surveillance planes took. The surface was riddled with what were obviously signs of urban life, even by alien definition. There were tall buildings with windows and tracks that resembled railways. It was possible he was wrong but there was clearly design and function involved. Someone or something was living or once lived on that ship, probably several thousand somethings. There were also no identifiable exhaust ports, waste expelling sites, or engines. And it floated miles above the ocean, still as a statue.

As a precaution, all overseas international travel was halted — officially. Unofficially, travel had been a thing of the past for all except the hyper-wealthy for several years. When petroleum and coal dwindled to trickles, major cities turned to solar, wind, and hydroelectric power, but the pivot had come too late to offset the depleted reserves. The U.S. military had sided with the scientific community about the environmental crises since the early 2000s, and Max Turpin was a huge part of that alliance sixty years later. But political will and dollar signs were stronger than an imminent existential catastrophe. While the world was in freefall, focus remained on personal freedom and eliminating threats to it. Whether those threats were real or imagined was irrelevant. It was true that the phrase "things are tough all over" could be used at almost any time, depending on point of view. These times were different.

Conservancy advocates said the wealthier nations had a decent water supply for its citizens, and it was true. But when someone has something that everyone needs, they better be ready to share it or defend it. Borders were overrun with thirsty and desperate people from neighboring countries. There was no stopping everyone when everyone needed water. But that didn't keep the larger nations of the world from trying.

The President of the United States, in conjunction with other select world leaders, had agreed to adopt a wait-and-see approach when it came to meeting the ship. They had attempted to contact it via telecommunications and radio. But just like radar and the satellites, when they sent a signal, there was no response. It was as if nothing was there. After a week of hand wringing and heated arguments, the world leaders decided that direct contact was the next and only option. Max Turpin was selected as the spokesperson for Operation: House Guest, the main objective of which was to establish communication with the ship and hopefully determine what its purpose was on Earth. Other countries seemed eager for the U.S. to risk its people and its meager resources on the task.

Turpin's background in science and support for research, regardless of how esoteric it might seem, made Turpin the natural choice. Most scientific research had been defunded for years, but Turpin continued to champion the notion that discovery was the way to salvation. "Technology will save us. It's the only thing that ever has," his wife Darla used to say, and he'd adopted that phrase as a mantra to keep her memory alive. Turpin was also the only military leader that was dead set against attacking the ship. Under no circumstances would he allow his planet to fire the first shot. But that didn't mean he would go unarmed. It was better to have a loaded gun and not need it than to Barney Fife a bullet.

Critics derided the president for squandering the country's remaining resources and thought that sending a show of force was asking for force in return. But Turpin felt that the ship was here for a reason, and he was going to find out what that reason was.

He activated ten out of the eleven aircraft carriers with a full contingent on each to sail for the giant ship. A byproduct of the global downturn was that able-bodied Americans had enlisted in the military en masse for the guarantee of food and shelter. It wasn't much, but it was more than what most people had. The recruitment had become so large that all military branches placed a moratorium on enlistment.

The fleet was humanity's last display of might. But with this much desperation packed into one place, any action could be provocation. Turpin needed to show strength without hostility. Presence without threat. Turpin wanted to get close enough for communication, but not so close as to seem aggressive. He gave the order to sail his ship underneath the visitors a few hundred yards from the colossal spire that sank into the water. Turpin figured that regardless of how close he was, the danger was the same. He wanted to see it up close.

Gwen informed him that the armada was in position, all crew members standing by. All pilots were in their jets. All weapons were loaded and staffed, and it was understood by all that no one would fire until ordered under penalty of court martial.

"Have we tried hailing it?" Turpin asked. His heart was nearly in his mouth, and he couldn't stop making fists with his fingers. Gwen sat staring at the ship high above them. The enormous craft seemed to swallow the sun. Even with all the lights on, it was still as dark as a cloudy moonless night sky. "Admiral?" Turpin said coolly. Gwen snapped her head from the ship.

"Yes. Sorry, Sir. All attempts to contact the vessel have been unsuccessful. It's like it's not even there," she said, sternly.

"Very well. Turn on the external speakers." His eyes remained fixed on the ship floating over him.

Gwen looked at the other officers and sailors on the bridge in confusion. They looked back with similar expressions.

"Sir," she said, "I would remind you that anything you say will be broadcast ship-wide. Everyone on board will hear you."

"Yes," Turpin said without looking away from the ship.

His second in command walked toward him with the bridge crew watching. She leaned in and spoke very softly. "Max, don't you want this conversation to be . . . well . . . private?" It was almost unheard of for the Rear Admiral to break protocol, especially in the presence of people in her command.

"No, Admiral. I don't," Turpin said with a scowl. "If I am to contact this visiting ship on behalf of the planet, the entire planet should hear what we say to each other. Now is not a time for secrets. Turn the speakers on."

Gwen didn't answer other than to give a salute and nod her head at the captain. She issued a series of orders to the sailors, and they repeated them in confirmation.

Turpin grabbed the transmitter and pressed the button to speak. It wasn't until that moment he realized what he was about to do. He wiped his sweaty palms on his pants and tried to swallow. His mouth was dry, and his head felt fuzzy. He closed his eyes and took a deep breath. It didn't help.

When he opened them again, he saw on the faces of the crew the same fear he felt. Their eyes asked the same questions he was. *Why are they here? What do they want? Who are they? What happens now?* Turpin stood up straight and gritted his teeth. For his crew, for everyone, he would not falter. He was about to be the first person ever to speak directly to intelligent life that was not of Earth.

He turned back to the ship in the air and spoke. "Visiting vessel, I am Admiral Maxwell Turpin of the United States of America. I am authorized by the people of Earth to welcome you." His voice reverberated over the dozens of speakers on the carrier. There was no reply. "You are the first non-terrestrial entity we have encountered. We attempted to contact you several times, but we do not know if you received our hails." Again, silence. The low hum of aircraft carrier motors was the only sound, but Turpin thought everyone could hear his heart thundering in his chest. The people on the bridge began to fidget, which meant other members of the crew were on edge too. He needed to get a response. "Please state the purpose of your arrival." A direct command. Risky and bold, but still friendly. "If you need assistance . . ."

"We have come to assist you." The words boomed like millions of voices through a megaphone; a sound Turpin could feel on his skin. He could almost smell it. The message had to be coming from the alien ship, but the sound permeated the air. He tried to think about how to respond, but he couldn't stop his legs from shaking. A squeeze surrounded the hand not holding the transmitter. Gwen stood next to him, holding it tightly. Turpin had no idea how long she'd been gripping his hand. He smiled at her and gently squeezed her hand back.

"While we appreciate you seeking us out, we require no assistance," Turpin said over the speakers.

"Prideful falsehood, Admiral Maxwell Turpin," the sound of a million voices said.

Turpin turned to his crew with a furrowed brow. The voice was right. Thousands of people had been massacred by standing armies ordered by their governments to prevent intrusion. Eventually, each nation saw the futility of murdering the anguished and opened their borders. Infrastructures imploded worldwide. Crime was rampant. Coastlines around the world had been forever altered due to melting ice caps.

Increased density meant increased use of resources. There simply wasn't enough to go around. Illnesses sprouted up in every corner of the globe as a result. Famine became widespread. Humanity had already tried saving itself through horror. On July 11, 2049, India initiated the Culling — killing every citizen over sixty to preserve resources. China, Nigeria, Indonesia, and others followed. In less than a year, 1.9 billion were gone, and it barely made a dent. Within a decade the world was back to starvation, disease, and talk of a second Culling. It wasn't exactly a mainstream subject, but it wasn't taboo anymore.

The Earth was on its way to ruin. Billions had already died.

Billions more would die in gruesome fashion. Turpin realized that whoever was on that ship understood the planetwide peril humanity was in, and that meant they had been watching.

"We have come to offer a trade," said the alien voice.

From its inflection, Turpin thought the voice sounded bored, like it had this conversation a thousand times before. He didn't see any point in trying to convince the visitors that Earth didn't need help. He was beyond trying to lie for the sake of ego. But he wasn't about to accept anything. Columbus was a trader too, and the New World might have been better off had they not accepted him.

"Thank you for the offer, but I am not in a position to negotiate any trade. Any deals you wish to make will be passed to my superiors with the understanding that . . ."

"We can fix your planet," the voice interrupted, like an entire population of people whispering directly into his ear.

Turpin opened his mouth to reply, but nothing came out. If he was being honest with himself, he wanted to hear more. The voice, almost as if sensing his desire, and probably the desire of everyone listening, continued. "We can cure all your diseases and prevent the onset of illness in the future. We will replenish your water to an infinite supply. We will repair your struggling atmosphere and clean your oceans. We will give you technology that will allow you to live the rest of your lives without want and in lavish comfort. We can turn your planet into a paradise."

Turpin looked around and saw many of his crewmen shaking. Was it apprehension? Joy? He looked out onto the flight deck and saw it was packed with almost every sailor onboard the aircraft carrier looking up to the ship. Some had their hands raised as if accepting manna from Heaven. Others were on their knees in supplicating gratitude. All were captivated. Turpin heard the crackle of the speakers and didn't realize he'd pushed the button to talk. "What would you want in return?" He hadn't meant to speak but couldn't stop himself.

The air thickened as the seconds passed without an answer. Turpin focused on the ship and the voice and nothing else. Time went on and to him, minutes, hours, days, centuries could have passed, and he wouldn't have noticed.

Slicing through the horrible silence that blanketed every person who could hear, the voice hissed. "We require the sterilization of every human."

No one said anything. The shock pressed on Turpin like an anvil falling from the sky. "You would all live your lives in comfort and security, but you will lose the ability to procreate. We will allow all females that are currently with offspring to birth their children normally. But they and their babies will be barren." The voice sounded like what it was offering, sterile.

"I do not have the authority to accept such a trade. What you are suggesting is . . ." Turpin paused, and the voice picked up where he left off.

"The extinction of your people. Yes. In exchange, your world will be healed. Do you accept?" The voice was nonchalant.

"I can't accept any offer you make. I don't have the authority," Turpin said. "We also have no proof that you possess the ability to do any of the things you claim." Turpin wasn't a negotiator, but he'd witnessed enough military negotiations to know not to tip his hand. He wiped his brow with a handkerchief from his pocket. It was sopping with sweat. He felt cold.

"We understand your hesitation," the voice said, accompanied by a mechanical whooshing noise coming from the ship, the first sounds it made since its arrival. Several thousand portals on the edge of the vessel started to open. Sailors screamed and began to back away. "Do not be alarmed. We will not harm you. We are releasing a reagent into your atmosphere that will be of great benefit to every member of your planet. It is our hope that this will prove our ability and our sincerity."

Light green smoke began to seep out of the thinnest part of the saucer. Almost as soon as it was released, it dissipated into nothing. When the smoke stopped, the portals closed with the same whooshing noise. The ship was silent again. "By this time tomorrow. The disease you call cancer will be eliminated, now and forever. Everyone who has contracted this disease will be cured, and no one will ever contract it again. It is gone."

Turpin dropped the receiver and put his hands on the window to steady himself. Gwen had done the same. Several members of the crew fainted. Turpin considered himself fortunate enough to be able to stay conscious. He pushed off the glass and fumbled for the transmitter. Sweat burned his eyes, and he struggled to clear them with the backs of his hands. He felt a trembling hand on his shoulder and saw Gwen trying to steady him as much as herself.

"I . . ." Turpin's voice cracked. "I have to report this to my superiors," he managed to squeak out. "And we must confirm your claim that you have cured . . ." He couldn't finish.

"We understand. We await your reply," the voice said in a blasé tone.

In a momentary burst of clarity, Turpin blurted out over the speakers, "How long do we have to make our decision?"

"Take as much time as you need," the voice said, but it was different. Stronger, almost menacing. "But know this, once you have made your decision, there can be no reversal. Whatever your choice, it will be permanent with no appeal."

With that, the conversation was over. The bridge crew was busy helping those who had fainted as they regained consciousness. Turpin ordered the fleet to maintain their positions and ready status until notified otherwise. They followed orders, though acted as if their minds were elsewhere.

Turpin and Gwen said nothing to each other as they walked together to his quarters. As soon as the door shut, Gwen made her way to Turpin's makeshift bar on the shelf and poured two very tall glasses of bourbon. Turpin collapsed into the office chair at his desk. Gwen sat on the bed and handed him the drink. He looked at her and tilted his head but took it and gulped half. They sat in silence for a while. Gwen took sips from her drink, rarely taking her eyes from the glass. Turpin stared straight ahead at nothing.

Gwen finally broke the tension. "You have to tell him."

"I have to tell everyone," Turpin said, not changing his gaze into oblivion, but he took a drink.

"Can it wait until tomorrow morning?" she asked. Turpin turned to her and smiled. She smiled back and shrugged. Turpin held out his nearly empty glass and Gwen clinked it with her own. "Let's have another. Then you make the call." She stood and reached for his glass. He drained it and gave it to her.

Gwen poured the drinks and Turpin looked at his hands. He stared at the plain gold band that symbolized his marriage. It was scratched and weathered, resting on his finger as a testament to a relationship that ended too early. Darla was buried with hers. "What would she say about all this?" he said, waving his hand in the air indicating everything.

Gwen handed him his glass full of rich brown liquid and sat back down on the bed. "She'd want to know how that ship is invisible to instruments."

Turpin nodded but continued. "No. I mean everything. The state of the world. All of it."

Gwen seemed to consider the question for a second and took a swig. "She'd be disappointed in us as a people, but she'd try to be positive about the future. She was like that to the end, if you remember."

He did remember. It also struck him that there was no future. "They killed her over groceries, and she would've given it to them had they asked." Turpin hadn't shed tears for his wife since she died, but the bitterness felt fresh. It always would. "What would you pick?" he asked, anger welling in his throat. "Would you take the deal?"

"Hang on, Max," Gwen said. "We don't even know if they — whoever they are — aren't bullshitting us. It could be a way to get us to drop our guard so they can make a move."

"Would she?" he asked.

Gwen emptied her drink in one gulp and turned the glass in her hand as if stirring her answer in it. "If you're asking me? Look at us. The most powerful nation in the world, floating on nuclear powered cities, and our people can't even take a shower. You know my niece doesn't even know what a full swimming pool looks like? And she never will. I read an article online on how to catch stray cats for food the other day. We're facing an agonizing death as a nation, as a culture . . . as a species." Gwen set her glass down. "I'd take the deal. Let's at least go out comfortably. It's the humane thing to do."

Gwen was not the kind of person to concede defeat to anything. Turpin understood her. Tomorrow didn't hold hope regardless of what choice was made. "You'd better get topside. Keep everyone prepared and make sure the fleet has a copy of the conversation with the visitor. I'll inform the president, and we'll debrief the captain on what the next move is when the president decides what to do."

Gwen nodded, stood, and made for the door. She put her hand on the handle and turned to her longtime friend. "By the way, Darla was a stubborn lady. She wasn't comfortable unless she was fighting for something." She looked Turpin straight in the face. "She'd say, 'Fuck that deal.'" Gwen opened the door and left.

Turpin took a few minutes to jot some points down on his report to the president. He also ordered a recording of the meeting to be sent to the White House. The president reacted exactly as Turpin thought he would: first shocked, then pensive, then irate, and finally asking his various advisors what to do. He was nothing if not predictable. The president ended the conversation with the diplomatic version of "Let's sleep on it." Maybe Gwen was right. Maybe Turpin could have waited until morning.

The next day came, but the darkness around the carriers was unchanged. Turpin only knew the passage of time by looking at clocks. No one slept. The crew had been ordered not to contact anyone about the events from the day before, but with so many people, a leak was unavoidable. By now the news of the alien message had traveled around the world.

Turpin didn't care. If he was ordered to find out who had done it, he would've said "Yes Sir!" and then ignored it. He was a loyal officer, but he wasn't going to spend his energy preventing the inevitable. There was no way to hide this, and Turpin didn't feel like anyone had the right to keep this confidential. Once reports of people being "miraculously cured", people put two and two together.

All around the world, people were claiming their cancer was not just in remission but totally gone. It was like they'd never been sick. Lung cancer, lymphoma, leukemia, carcinoma all of it, gone. People on their death beds celebrated with family. Pediatric wings of overwhelmed hospitals were filled with parents hugging and kissing their children. The unconquerable disease that plagued humanity since its inception was totally eradicated in a day.

Many people believed the cure was divine intervention. Considering the state of the planet and the thinning of hope, Turpin understood why people would reaffirm their faith. It was possible the visitors were something akin to gods. They didn't boast, and they weren't joking. There were skeptics in the world though, and he thought it was at least prudent to be so, considering what was on the table. But like Gwen had said, either way, the people of Earth were going down. This — the cure for cancer — was the extraterrestrial version of a parlor trick. Like a drug dealer, it was a taster to get the planet to buy more product.

After a few hours of continuous global reports of inexplicable healing, the president contacted Turpin. The red phone blinked indicating there was an emergency and Turpin was required to answer. He was also required to have a witness. Gwen stood by him and nodded in support. "Yes, Mr. President," Turpin said like a good soldier, turning on the speaker function.

"Hello, Max," the president said in his lazy Southern way. "Sleep OK?"

"No, Sir. You?" Turpin said.

"Not a wink." The president said something unintelligible to someone in the room with him. "They weren't lyin'. It's gone."

"No. Sir. They weren't lying."

There was a pause as the president spoke again to others in the room with him. "Max, I won't blow smoke. What I'm about to tell you is top secret, the highest of security clearance. I know Gwen is probably in there with you?"

"Yes Sir, Mr. President. I'm here," she said.

"Good." He took a deep breath. "Admirals, the global situation is worse than anyone in the media reports or realizes. Our best guess puts our water supply totally unpotable in nine years. Which means we've run out of ways to grow food. We've gotta shut down sewage systems and waste treatment. We think" — he emphasized 'think' as if to insinuate he didn't believe it himself — "we could last another five or so years after that, but that's it. We're looking at biological insolvency in less than twenty years." An eerie quiet stretched out over everyone on the line, and Turpin felt as if everyone in the world was listening, holding their breath.

"Sir." Turpin broke the silence. "Are you saying you want to take the deal?" He cut to the chase. Turpin didn't want to drag this out. He looked at his second, and her face was like stone.

"Admiral, I'm telling you we're done for either way. In four days, I was going to enact an executive order that limited electrical use for everyone to one hour a day, per household. We had a good run, but it's high time we take our medicine. There's a price to pay for every choice. And the bill is due." Then, through a muffled sob, the president said, "I'm ordering you to accept the deal. You're authorized to speak to them and agree to their terms. There are media crews headed to meet you as we speak to cover and record the event for the world to see. I expect it to be done tonight."

"Yes." Turpin gathered what little strength he had left. "Yes, Sir."

"Hey, Max. We weren't going to make it anyway," the president said, forcing a chipper attitude. Always the politician. "We won't forget your part in all this."

But he would. Everyone would. Nothing anyone has ever done, was doing, or might do would be remembered. Turpin gulped the bile rising in his throat from the thought. He didn't reply.

"Let me know," the president said, and the line went silent for good.

Turpin turned to Gwen. They said nothing but embraced each other as friends do when they say goodbye. And Turpin thought to himself that it was goodbye in a real visceral way, it was goodbye to all.

The flight deck of the USS Gerald R. Ford was teeming with cameras and journalists sent to cover the acceptance of the trade: Paradise for extinction. Social media polls overwhelmingly favored taking the trade. All the remaining major nations threw their support behind accepting the deal. The world it seemed was going to die peacefully without suffering and without a fight.

Turpin stood on the bridge with the same crew as when they'd arrived with the idea of a fight banging around in his head. What was there to fight? The enemy was humanity's indifference and selfishness. *How does anyone fight against that?* He banished the idea from his mind. He had one last job to do. As he held the transmitter, he vowed to himself that it would be the last time he followed orders from anyone. As soon as he was done, he would resign his command.

All eyes were on him as he clicked the microphone on. Turpin looked up and expected to see blinking lights or banners or something from the giant ship other than stoic stillness and silence. He thought that whoever was inside was acting as if they'd gone through this part of the deal hundreds of times.

Turpin was determined to accept the deal, but he wanted

answers. As the authorized spokesperson for every human on Earth, he figured that entitled him to some privilege, and he planned to use it. "Visiting vessel," he said through the speakers with more confidence than he felt. "We have come to a decision."

The ship hummed and vibrated for the first time, like it was energizing itself. "And what have you decided?" the single voice made of many said.

"I have questions that will not influence the choice I have been ordered to make. But . . ." He cleared his throat. "There are things I want . . . I need to know from you." He saw the red phone blinking. The president would tell him to take the deal and move on. "How long will the process take for you to . . . for the world to be fixed?"

"Approximately one week." The answer was curt and immediate.

"Will anyone be harmed during this procedure?" Turpin said. Gwen held up a sheet of paper with the words *Are you looking for a fight?* written on it. He wasn't looking to fight the visitors. But when he saw the note, he steeled himself to continue his questioning. The red phone was still blinking.

"Admiral," the communications officer said. "I have the White House demanding to speak with you." Turpin ignored it. The world was ending. What could they do to him now?

"No," the voice answered. "No living being on your planet will be harmed."

"What will you do with our planet when we are gone?" Turpin said in a defiant voice. A fighting voice. "That is what you want isn't it? But you won't do the dirty work yourselves. You won't kill us. That's what you do. You find worlds that are on their last legs and offer them paradise to die and then you take over. We simply fade away, fat and happy. Capricious pacifists!"

The humming got louder, and the air grew heavy with energy. The hairs on everyone's arms stood up. The lights got brighter. "Admiral Maxwell Turpin." The voice was huge now and spoke with primal force, "Do your dinosaurs ask what you are doing with your planet? Do any of the species your people eliminated ask? When it is your time, there is no going against it. What do any of you care what happens to your world? After all the harm you have done to yourselves, you have the nerve to accuse us of cruelty? Your people have destroyed themselves. You cannot fight the end."

The memory of something said to him the day before slammed into him harder than the million voices of one. *She wasn't comfortable unless she was fighting for something. She was a champion for science. She lived her life promoting ideas.*

"She'd say, 'Fuck that deal,'" Turpin whispered to himself. He thought of Darla and everything she never saw. He thought of the children he never had with her. The house they never bought. The dog they never rescued from the pound. He thought of the life he never got the chance to live and regretted the one he had.

"What have your people decided?" the voice was back to being unconcerned. "We will remind you that the choice you make is irrevocable. There will be no second chances."

"I understand," Turpin said but the button to turn on the speakers wasn't pressed.

"Max?" Gwen said. And looked at him with sorrow in her face. "Don't," she whispered.

Staring at her he pressed the button "We have decided to decline your deal. We appreciate your offer and thank you for your visit."

The rumble from the ship died out and the voice said, "Very well." The two thin spires retracted into the ship, and it lifted away from the water without a sound. As it did, the sun shone on the carriers, bright and beautiful in the cloudless blue sky. The alien ship was gone. Everyone watching from all ten vessels stared at the sky in collective confusion. The look on each person's said, *Did that just happen?*

Max Turpin didn't wait to be arrested. He surrendered himself to Gwen almost as soon as the ship was out of sight. She escorted Turpin to the brig with her sidearm out and announced that she would personally shoot and throw overboard anyone who even talked about hurting the prisoner. That's what she called him.

They made it to the brig and Turpin walked in without protest. Gwen shut the door and turned to leave. The look on her face was a combination of apology and rage.

"I did it for her," Turpin said. "I wanted to give us something to fight for." Gwen shook her head and walked out.

"The trial was short," Dr. Eckhart said to the students in his classroom. "Turpin said before he was even charged that he would plead guilty. They had trouble with that, because technically there was no crime for what Turpin had done other than disobeying orders. They settled on treason which was punishable by death at that time. Max Turpin was executed by lethal injection 214 years ago today."

The children tapped on their pads furiously taking notes. "That one individual act of defiance led to our salvation," Dr. Eckhart said. Hands all over the classroom went up and he motioned for them to be put down. "In refusing the president's order, he forced us to examine all the mistakes we'd made. That alone would not have been enough, but when the visitors departed, they left the cure for cancer behind. The reagent that eliminated it was still in the air.

Turpin's longtime friend, Gwen Hernandez-Chase was smart enough to realize this and forced the United States government to throw their full weight behind researching and investigating the alien cure. What did they have to lose? That research led to the discovery of waste dissolving. We no longer needed water for waste disposal. More research led to more discoveries. And we find ourselves here today, in a world free of disease and living in peace . . . for the most part. That's why August 8th is Max Turpin

Day." The lecture went on until the chimes rang for the end of the school day.

The children ran out welcoming their various games and friends and snacks and everything else that children welcome after school. They ran past a statue of an unassuming man in an old military uniform. The inscription under it read "Fight for something. -Admiral Maxwell Turpin."

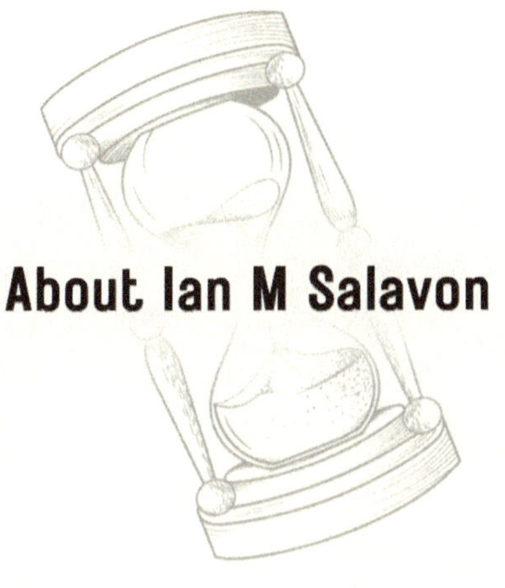

About Ian M Salavon

Ian is a husband, father, professional chef by trade, wannabe Renaissance Man, and longtime aficionado of speculative fiction. When Ian is not cooking, hanging out with family or writing, he spends his free time at the Fort Worth Judo Club where he is a black belt and coach. Ian has short stories published in On The Premises Magazine, www.kaidankaistories.com, and Small World City in Feb. 2025, but most of his work is featured in long road trips and around the dinner table. You can read more of Ian's work at www.shortstorysalavon.com

Twitter and Bluesky: @SalavonIan

Also by WriteHive

If you enjoyed *Surviving Humanity*, please consider reading our other Anthologies in the series: Rescuing Curiosity, Reclaiming Joy, and Navigating Ruins. As with all WriteHive Anthologies, all profits from these books are directly donated to WriteHive.

We also appreciate any and all reviews! You may leave a review on Goodreads, Amazon, IndieStoryGeek, or on our site at Inkedingray.com

You can learn more about WriteHive at writehive.org or on our socials (Instagram, Threads, Facebook, and BlueSky) at @write_hive

Thank you so much for reading!

www.ingramcontent.com/pod-product-compliance
Lightning Source LLC
Chambersburg PA
CBHW021330190726
48288CB00003B/1039